8-22-13

D0914739

Dear Parent:

Psst . . . you're looking at the Super Secret Weapon of Reading. It's called comics.

STEP INTO READING® COMIC READERS are a perfect step in learning to read. They provide visual cues to the meaning of words and helpfully break out short pieces of dialogue into speech balloons.

Here are some terms commonly associated with comics:
    PANEL: A section of a comic with a box drawn around it.
    CAPTION: Narration that helps set the scene.
    SPEECH BALLOON: A bubble containing dialogue.
    GUTTER: The space between panels.

Tips for reading comics with your child:

• Have your child read the speech balloons while you read the captions.
• Ask your child: What is a character feeling? How can you tell?
• Have your child draw a comic showing what happens after the book is finished.

STEP INTO READING® COMIC READERS are designed to engage and to provide an empowering reading experience. They are also fun. The best-kept secret of comics is that they create lifelong readers. **And that will make you the real hero of the story!**

Jennifer L. Holm and Matthew Holm
Co-creators of the Babymouse and Squish series

For Ravi

RHUS29255

 Published in the United States by Random House Children's Books, a division of Random House, Inc., 1745 Broadway, New York, NY 10019, and in Canada by Random House of Canada Limited, Toronto.

Visit us on the Web!
StepIntoReading.com
randomhouse.com/kids
dckids.kidswb.com

Educators and librarians, for a variety of teaching tools, visit us at RHTeachersLibrarians.com

ISBN 978-0-449-81616-5 (trade) – ISBN 978-0-449-81617-2 (lib. bdg.) –
ISBN 978-0-449-81618-9 (ebook)
Printed in the United States of America
10 9 8 7 6 5 4 3 2 1

STEP INTO READING®

STEP 2

DC SUPER FRIENDS™

A COMIC READER

CATCH CATWOMAN!

By Billy Wrecks

Illustrated by Erik Doescher, Mike DeCarlo,
and David Tanguay

Random House 🏠 New York

It’s a quiet night in Gotham City.

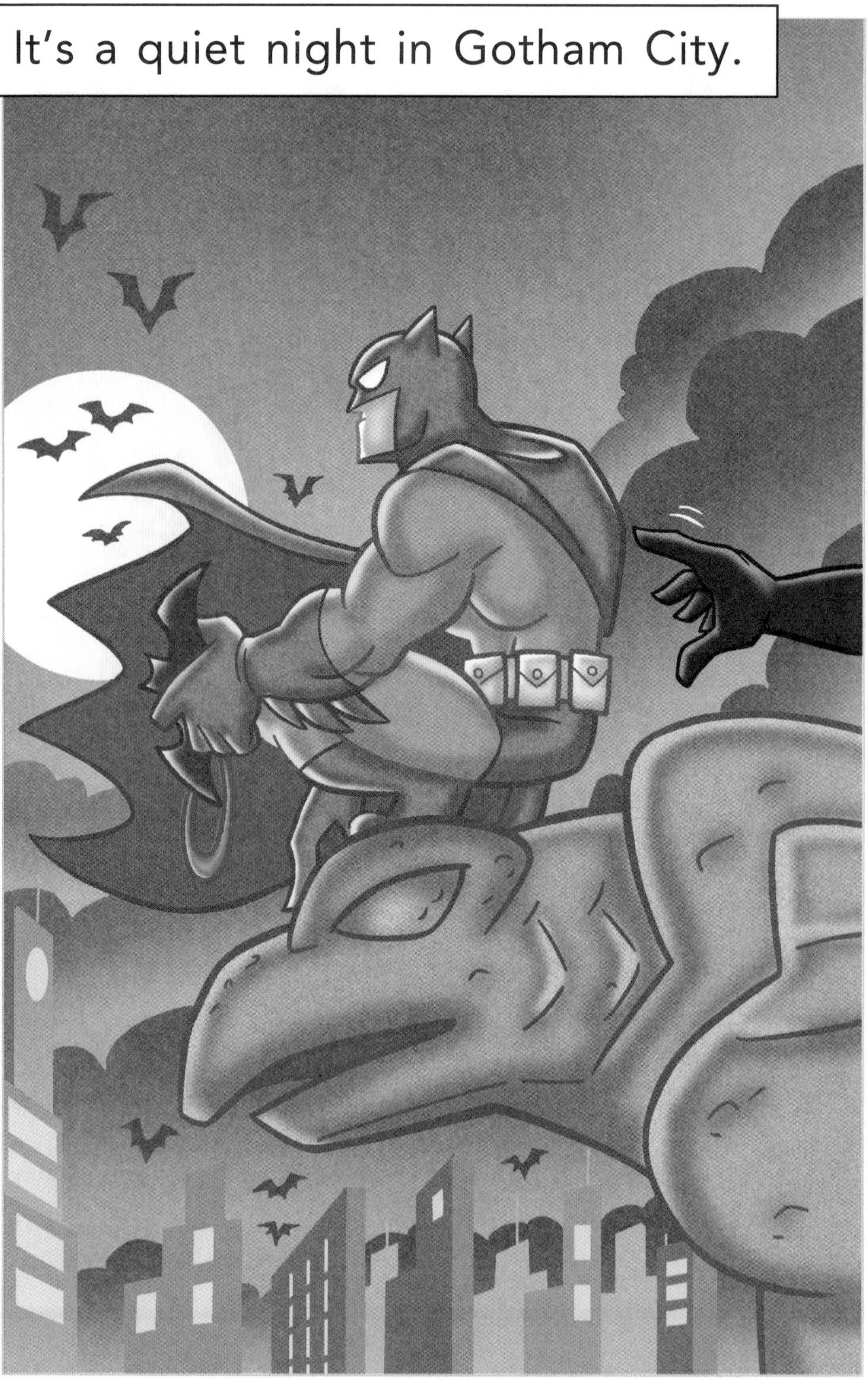

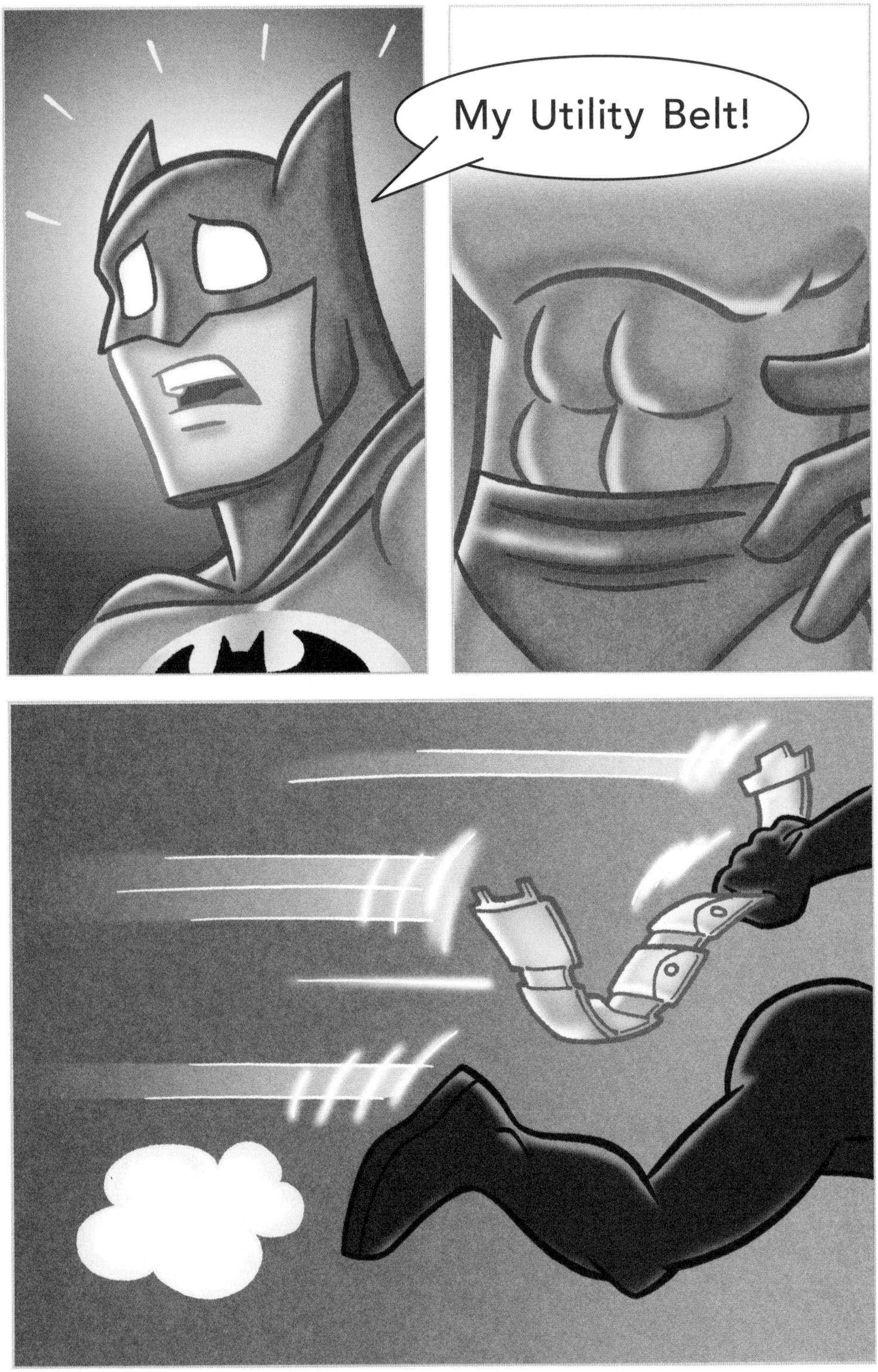
My Utility Belt!

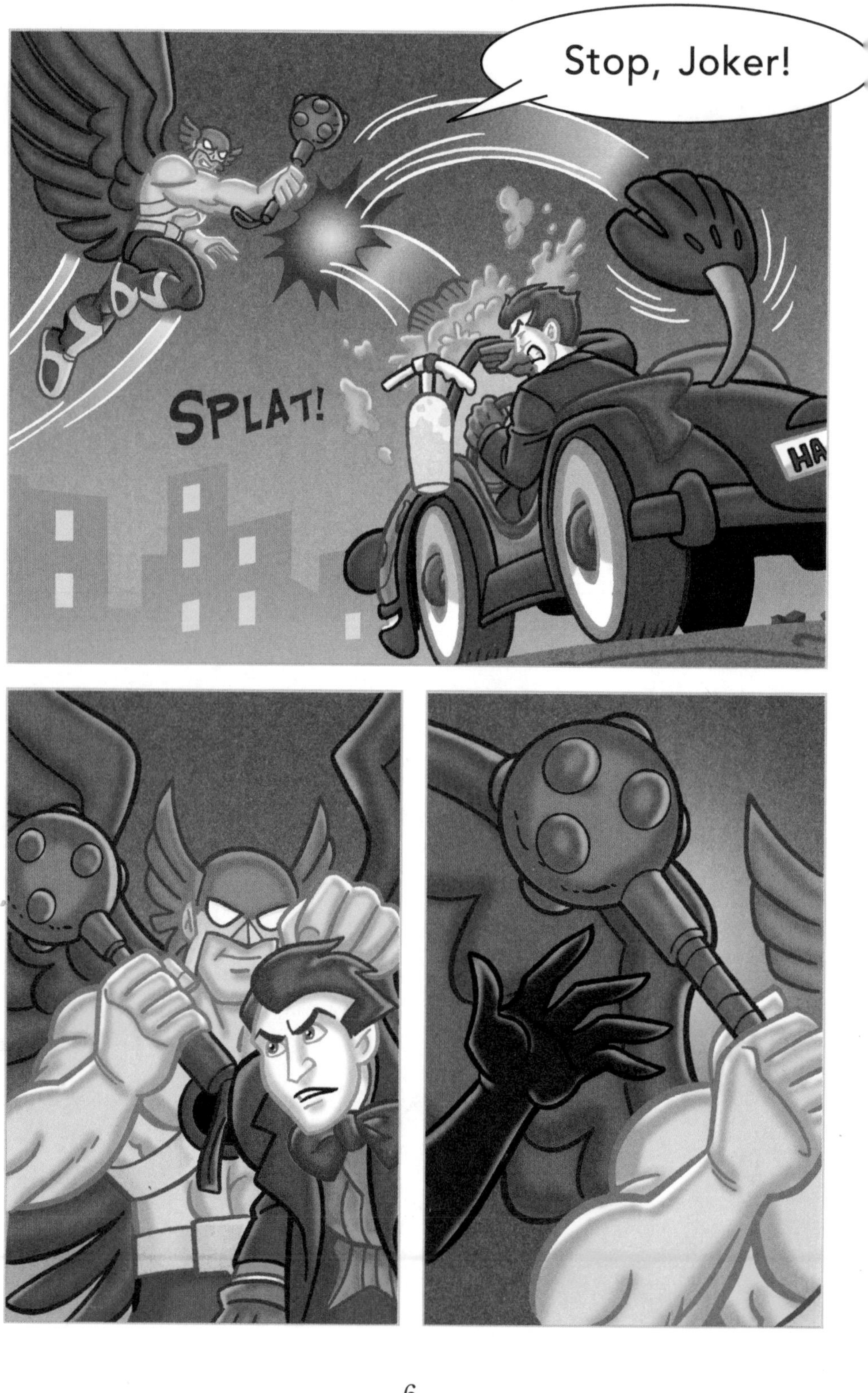
Stop, Joker!
SPLAT!
HA

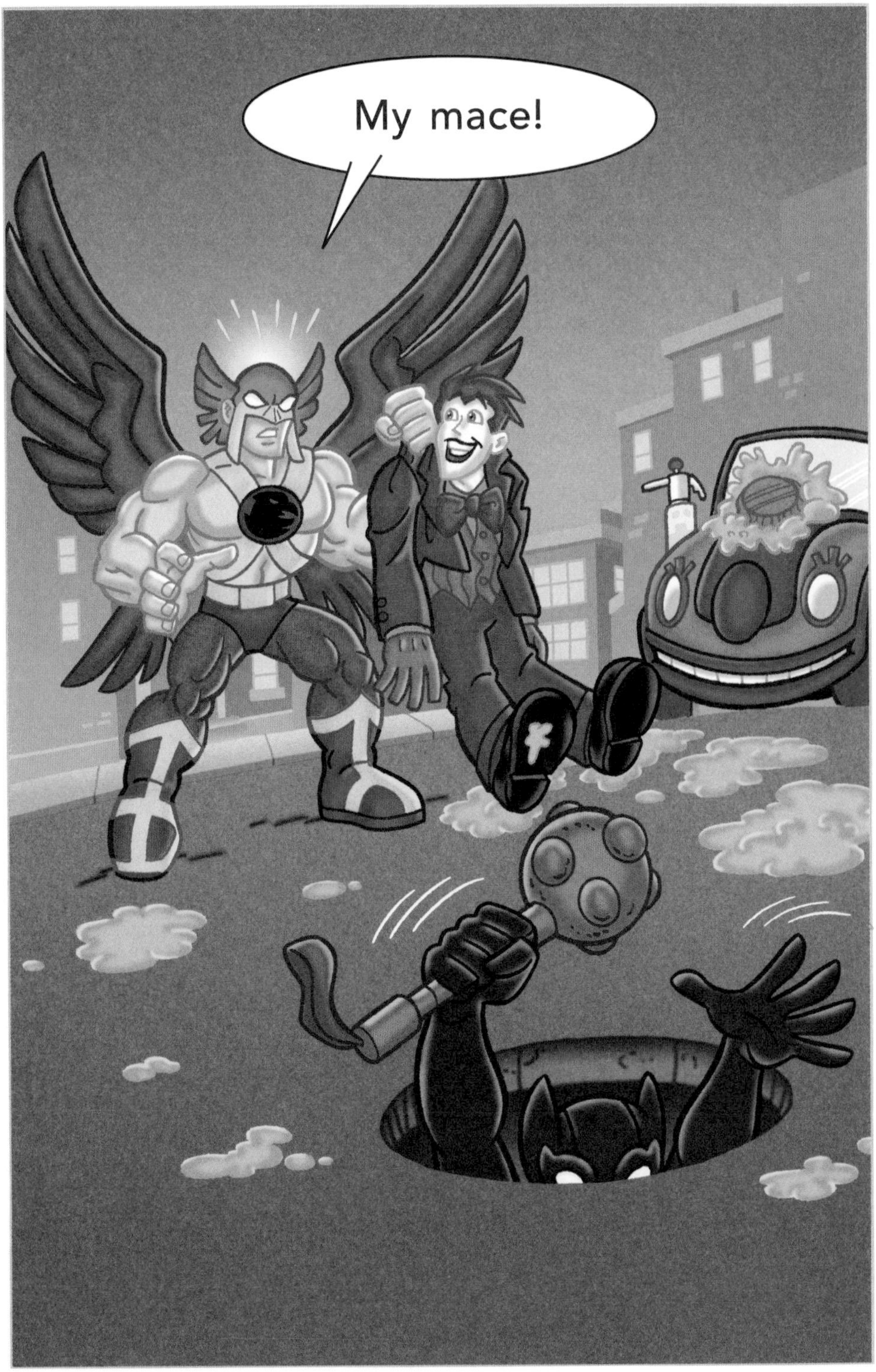
My mace!

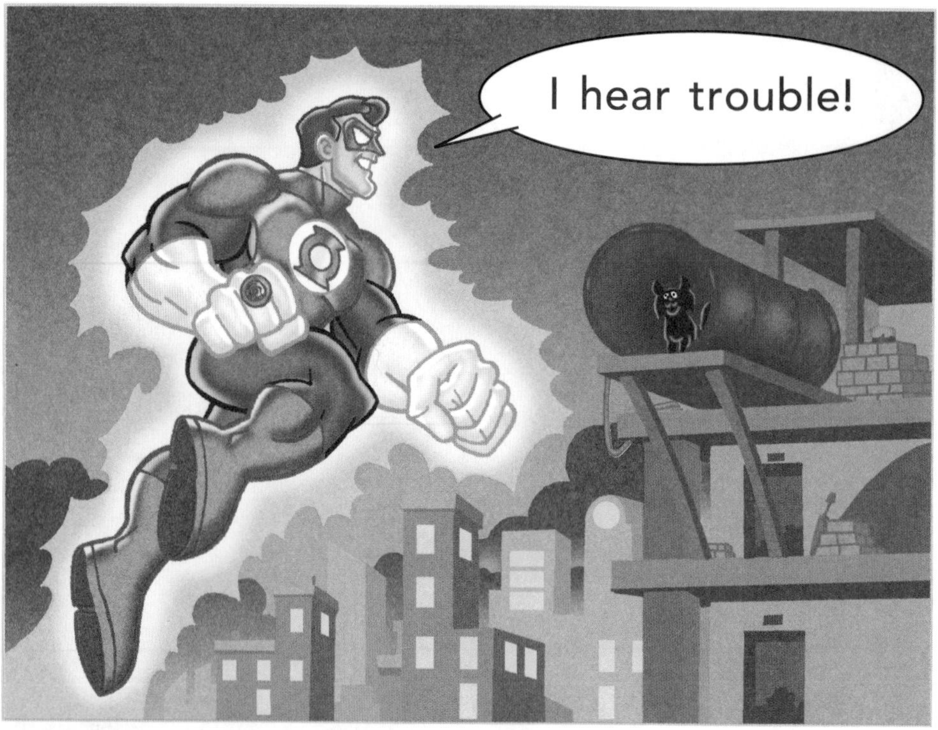
I hear trouble!

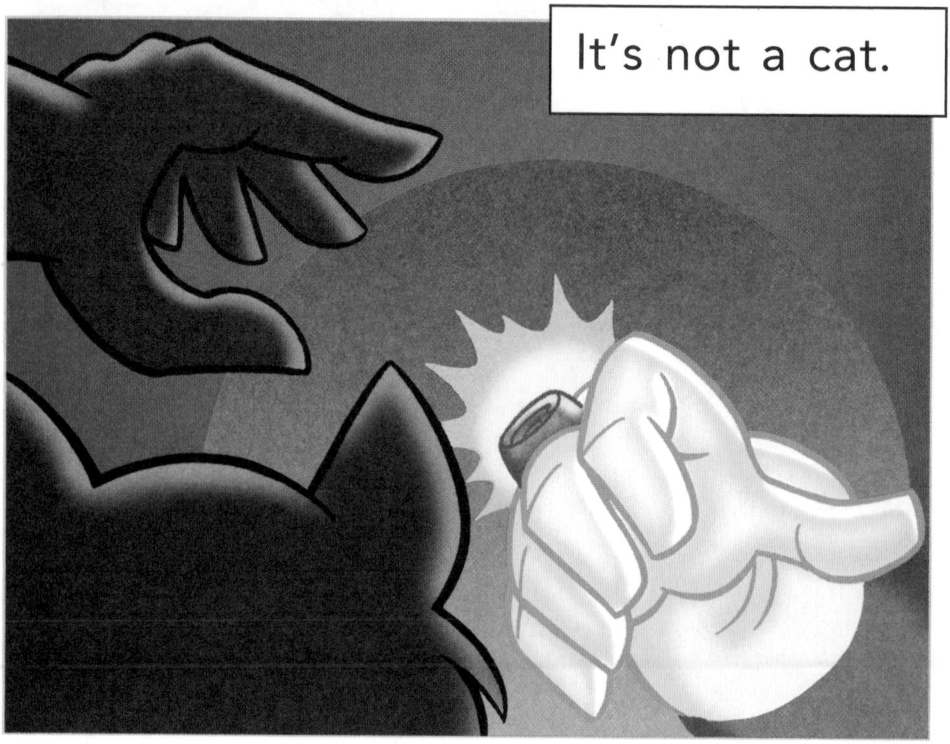
It's not a cat.

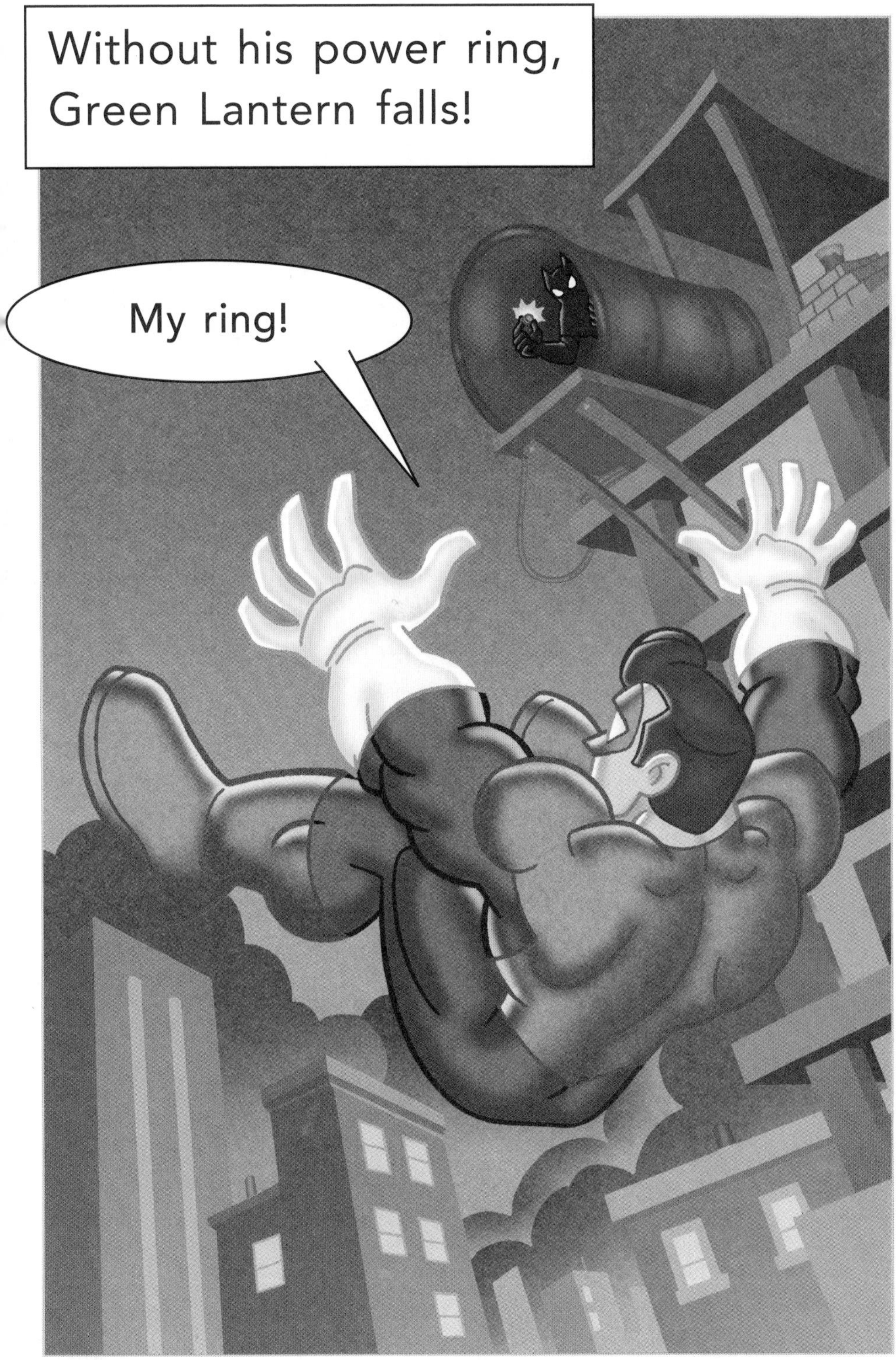
Without his power ring, Green Lantern falls!
My ring!

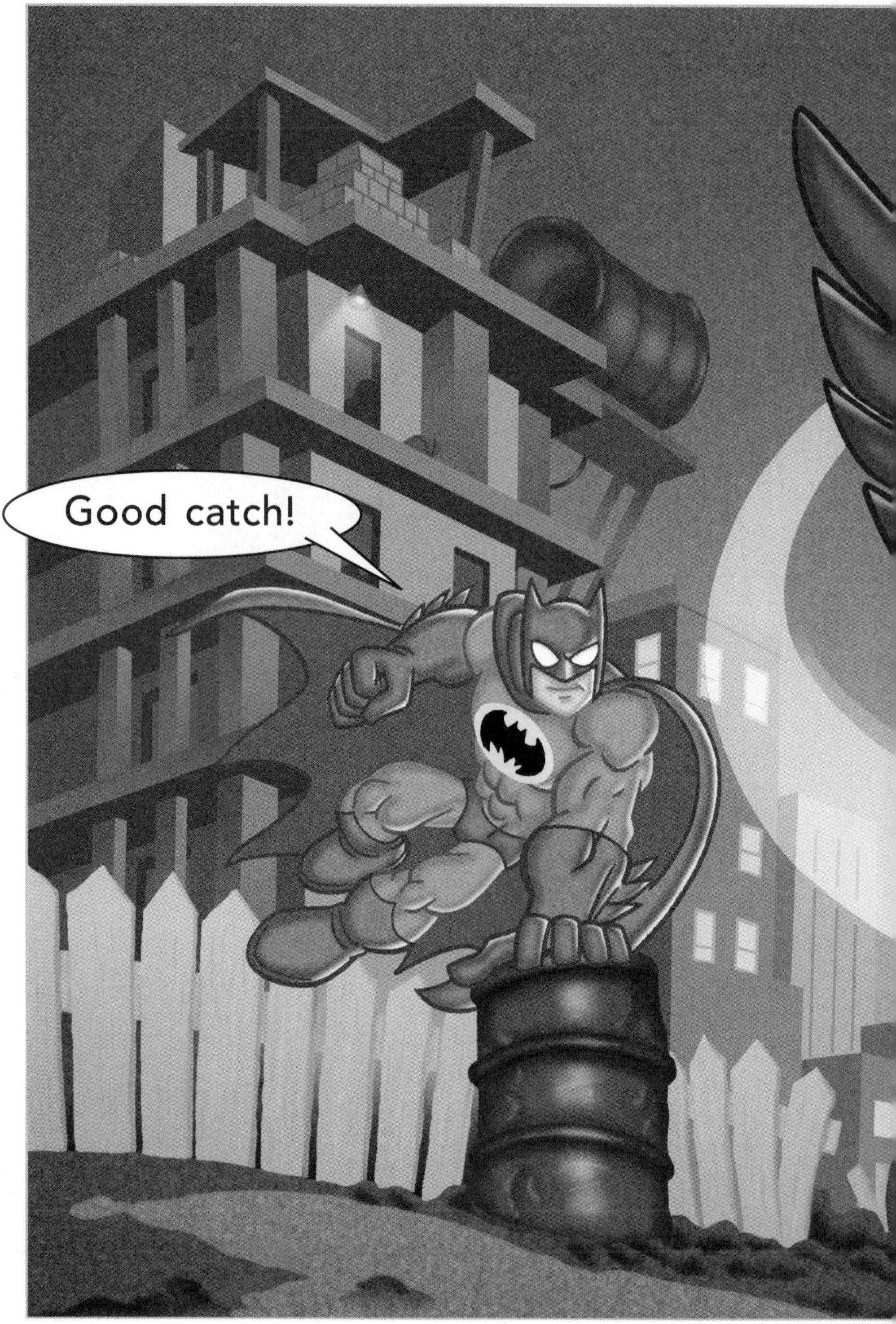
Good catch!

Hawkman flies
to the rescue.

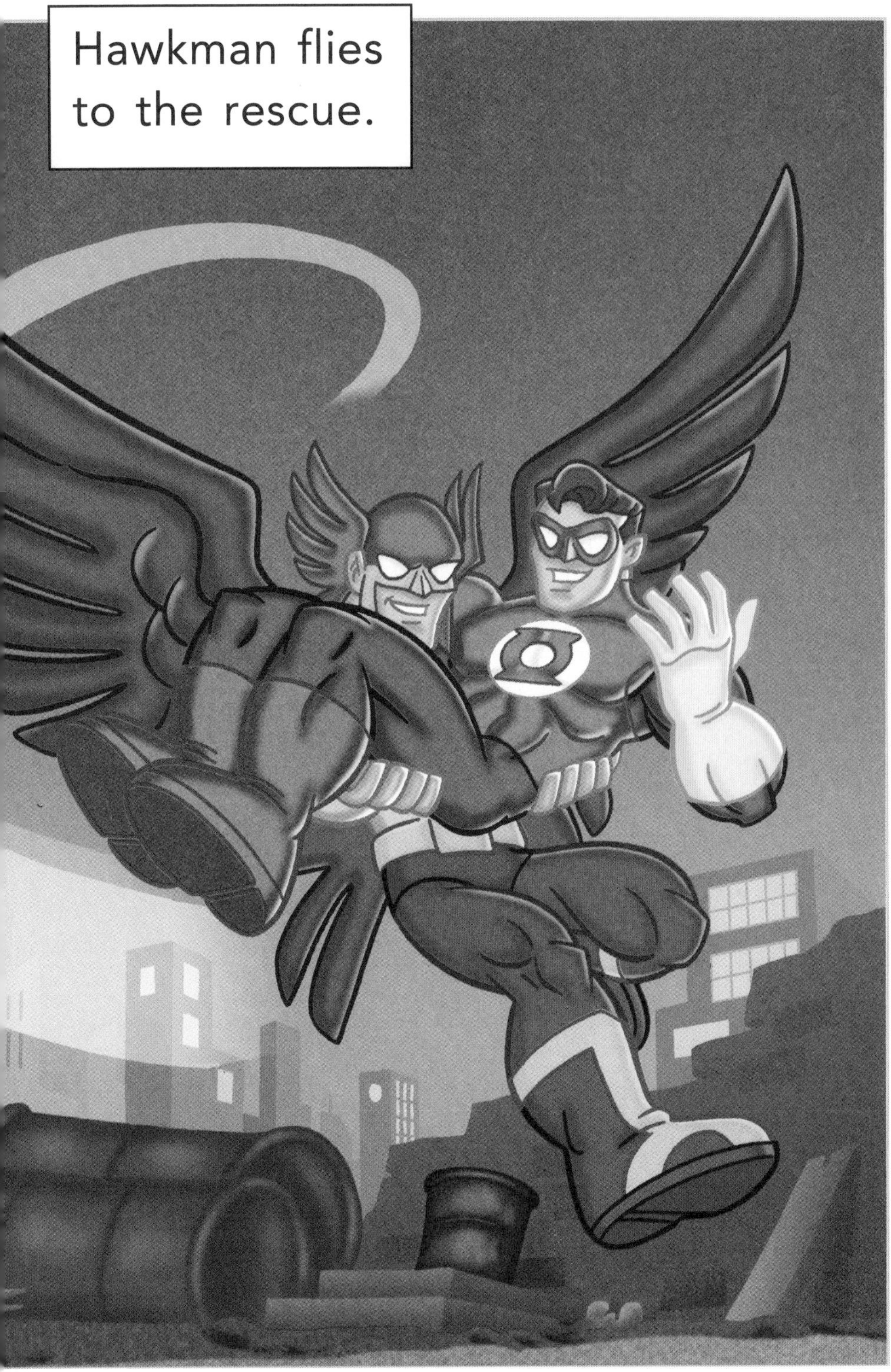

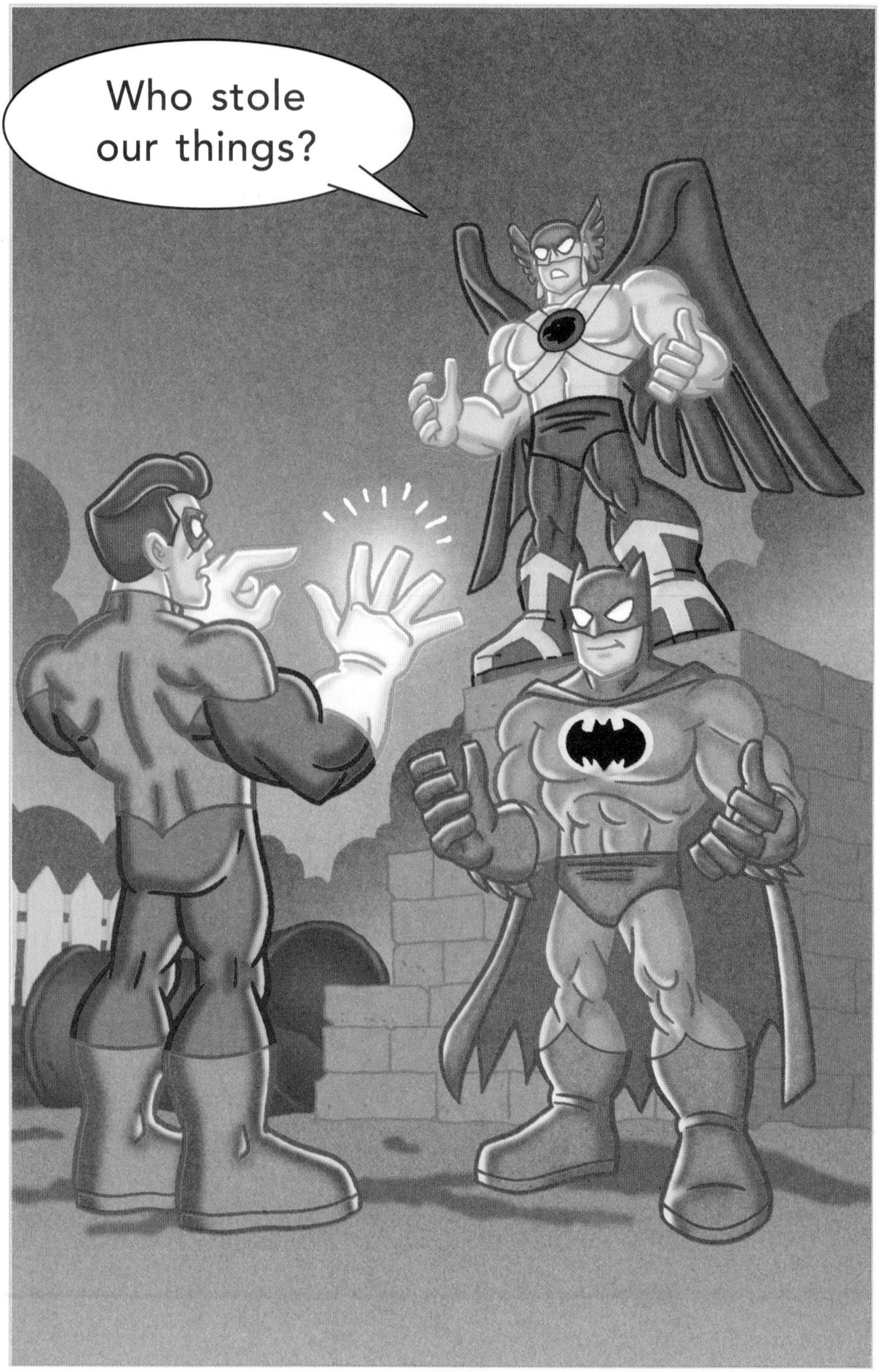
Who stole our things?

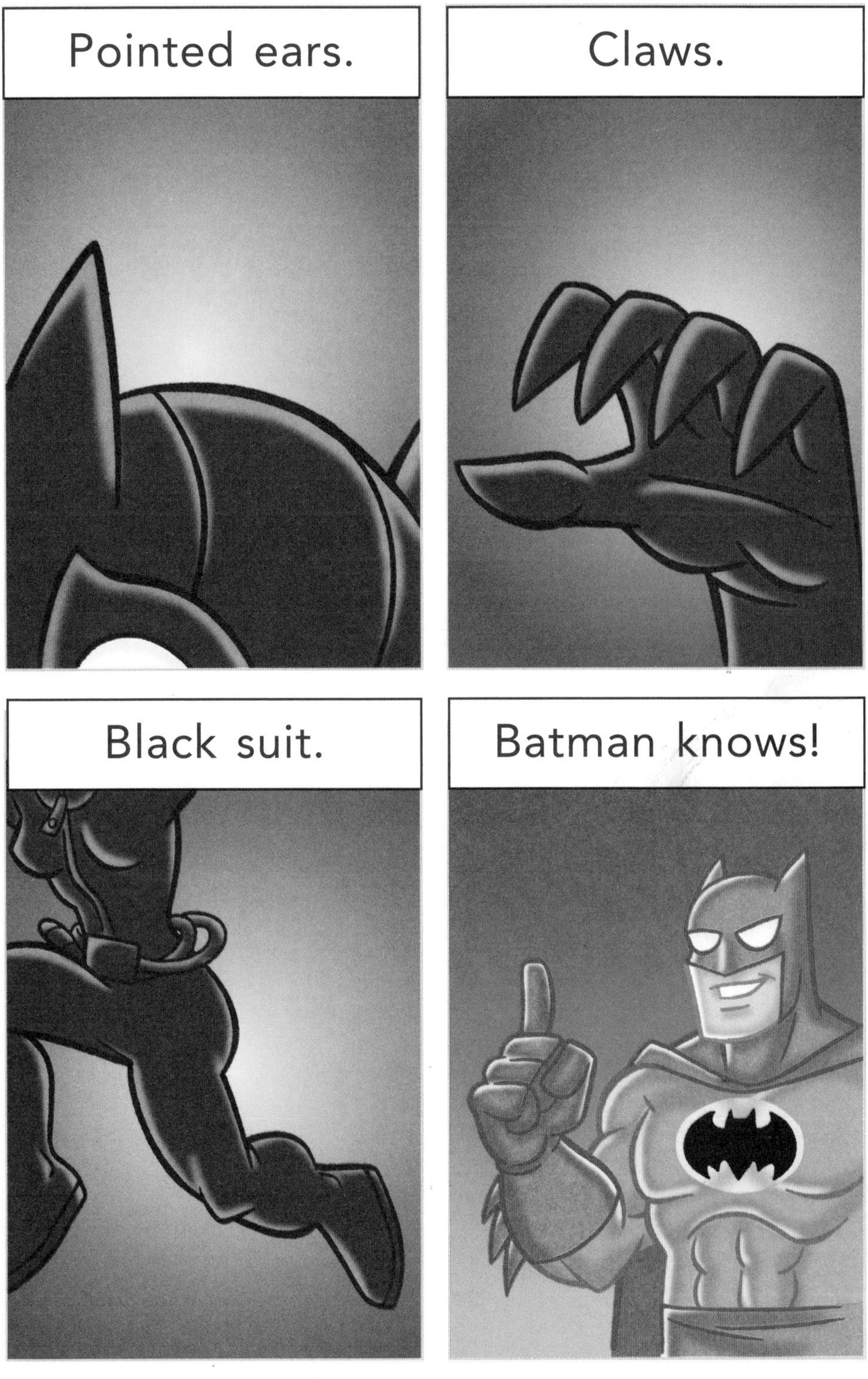
Pointed ears.
Claws.
Black suit.
Batman knows!

Catwoman!

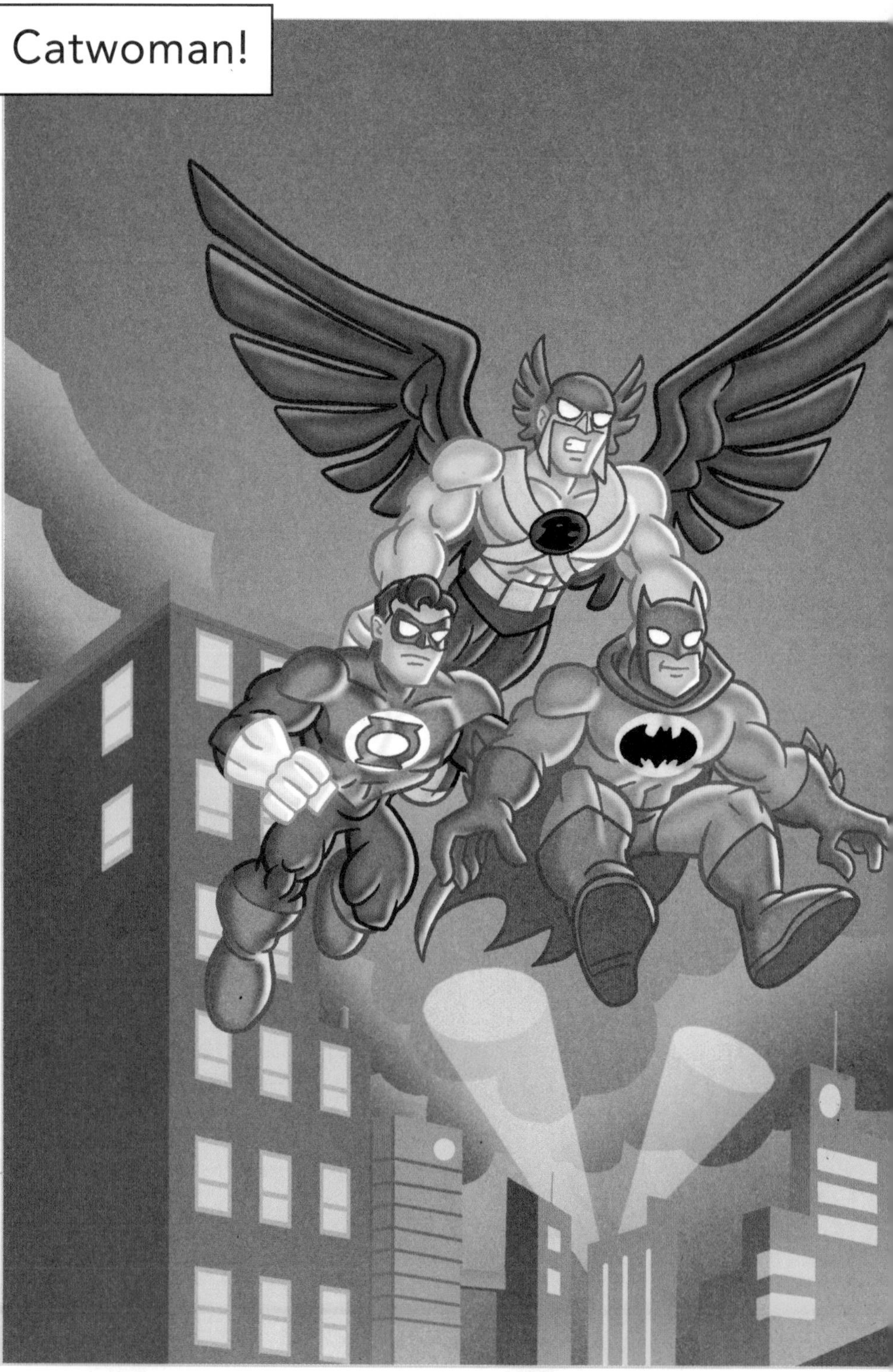

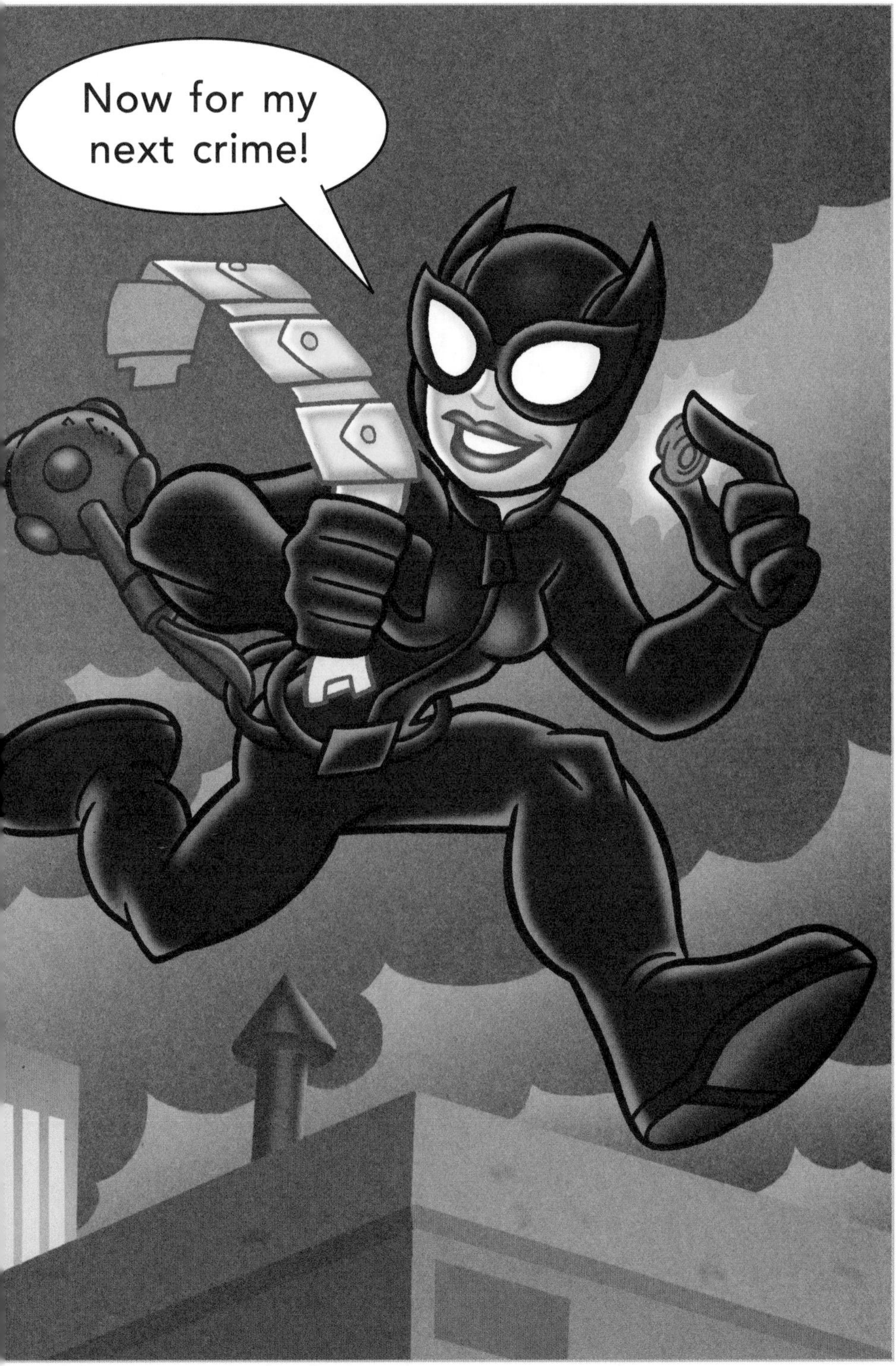
Now for my next crime!

Catwoman sneaks
into the cat show.

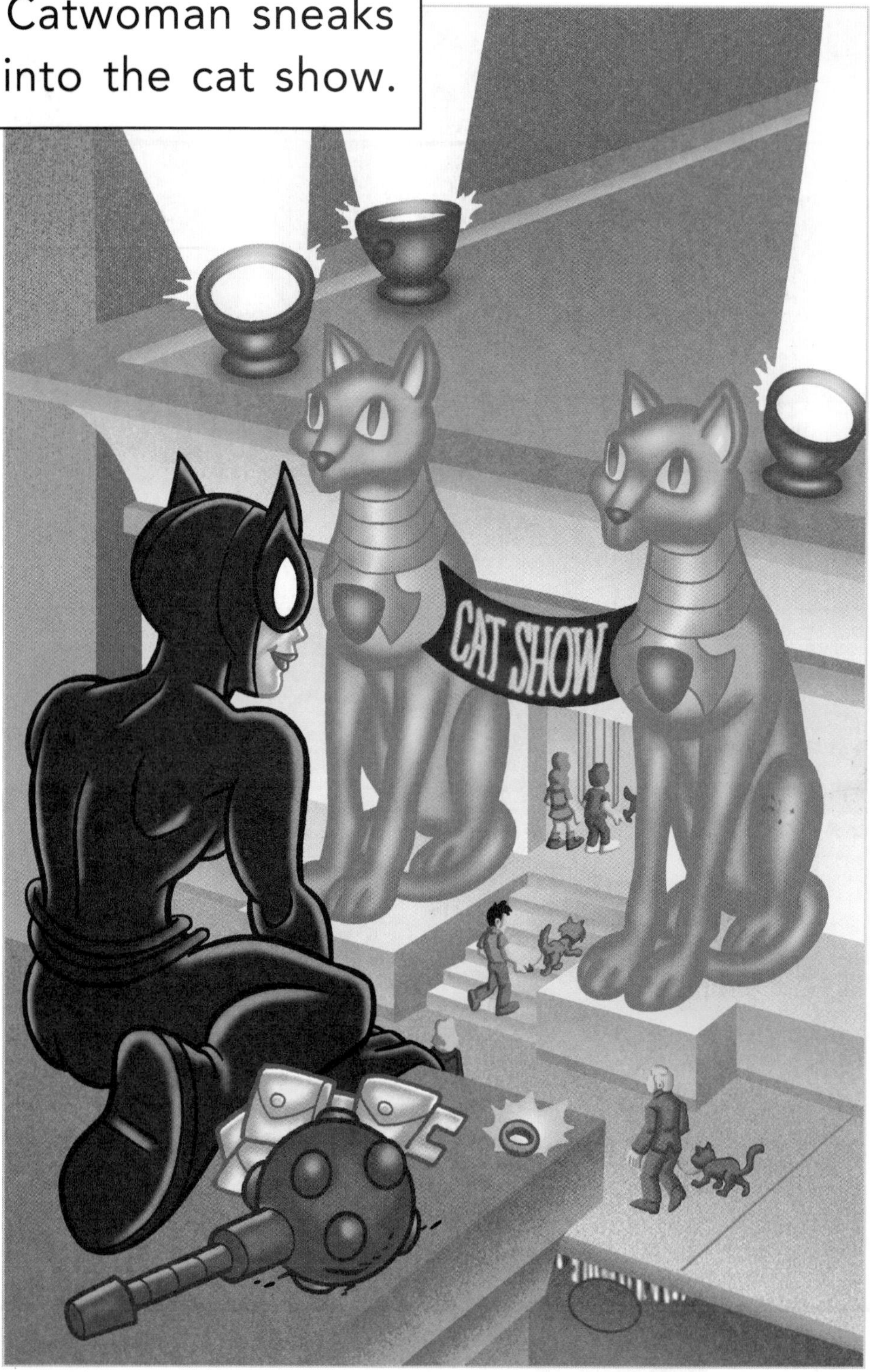
CAT SHOW

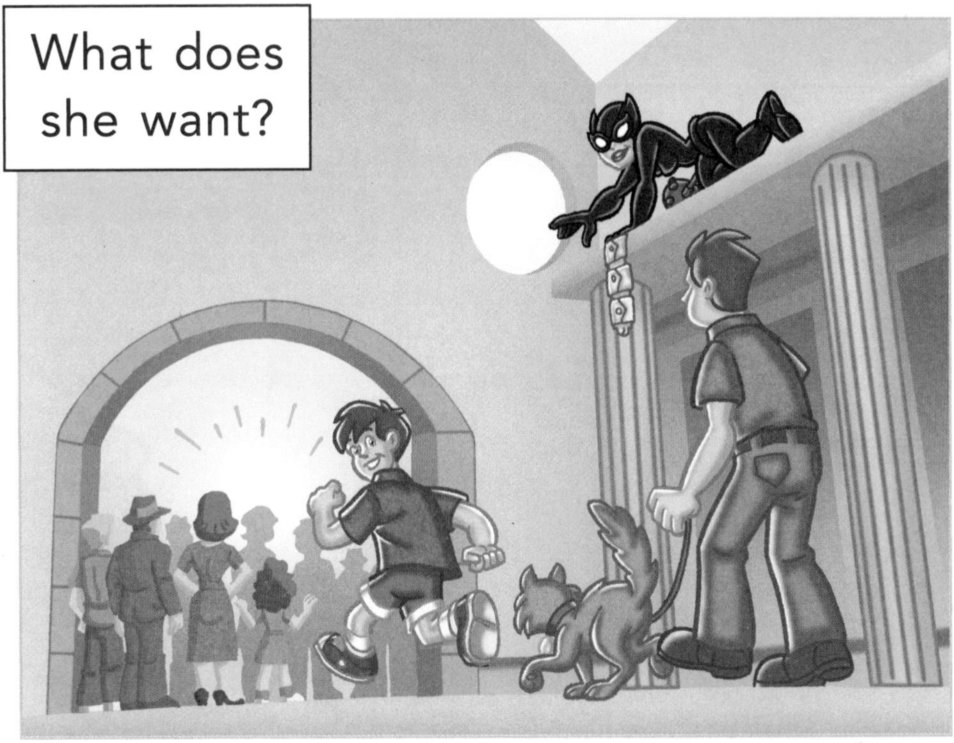
What does she want?

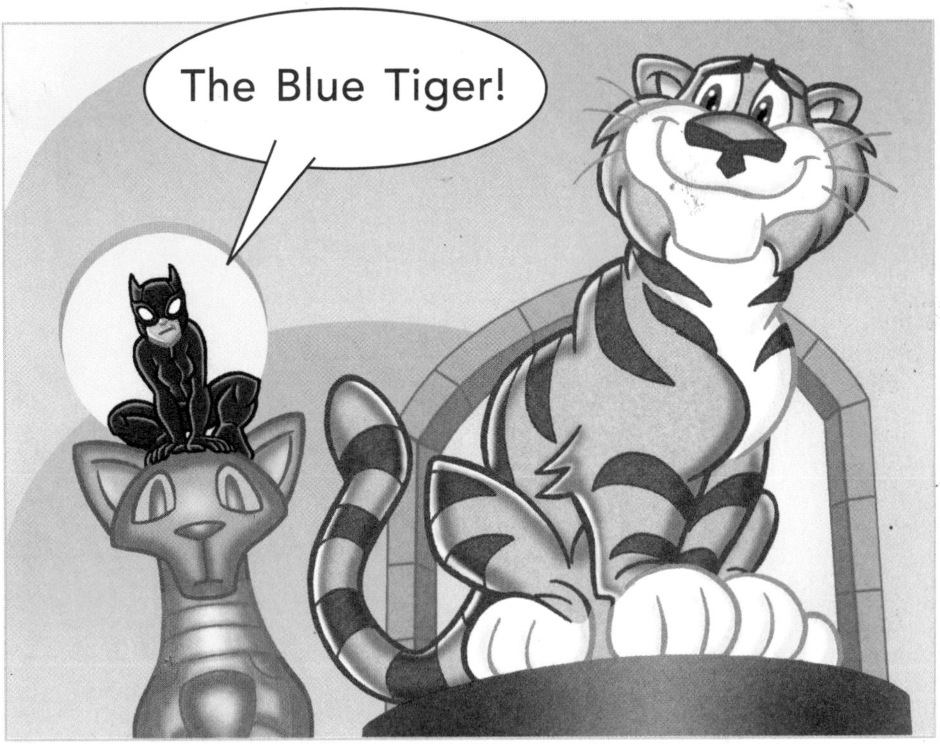
The Blue Tiger!

The Blue Tiger is one of a kind.

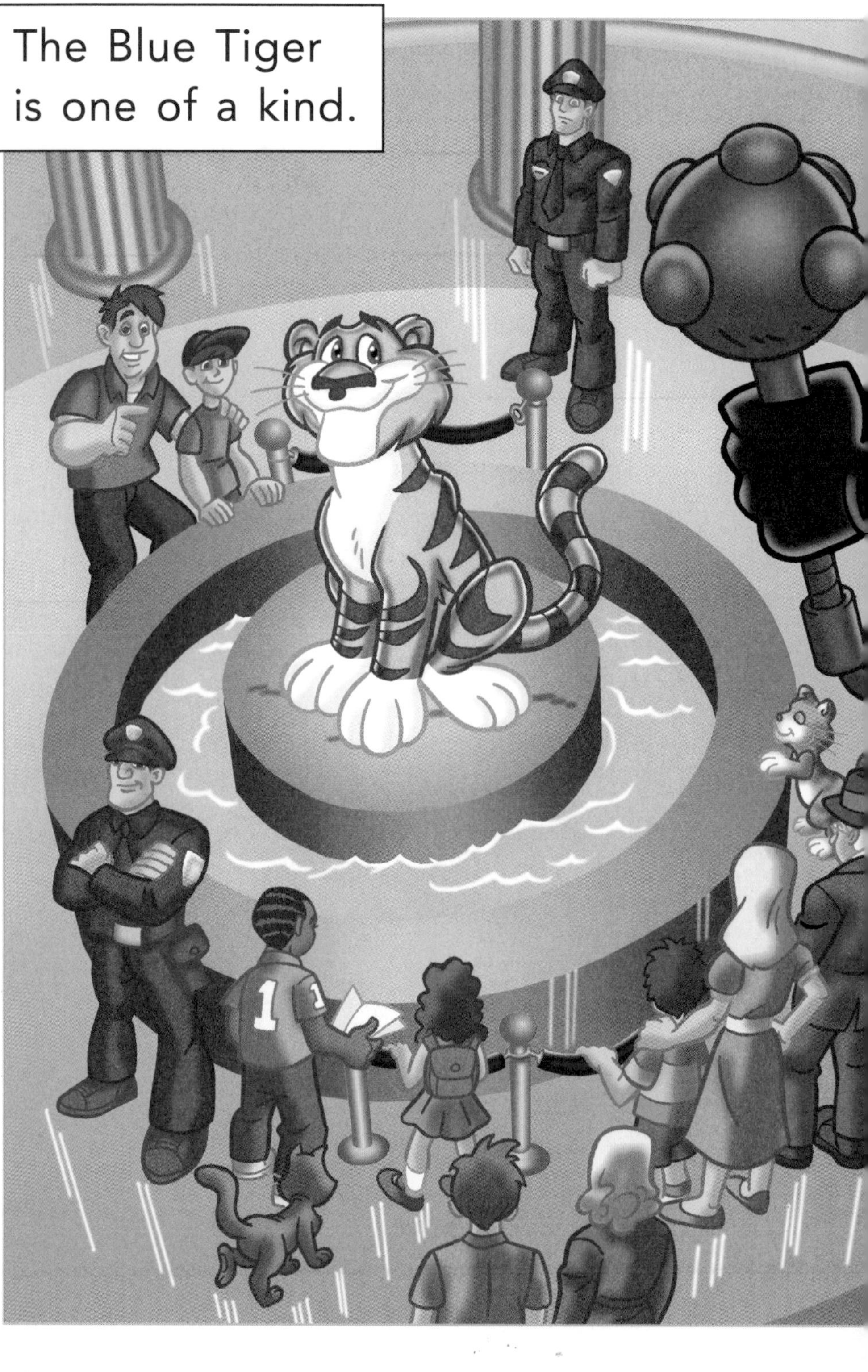

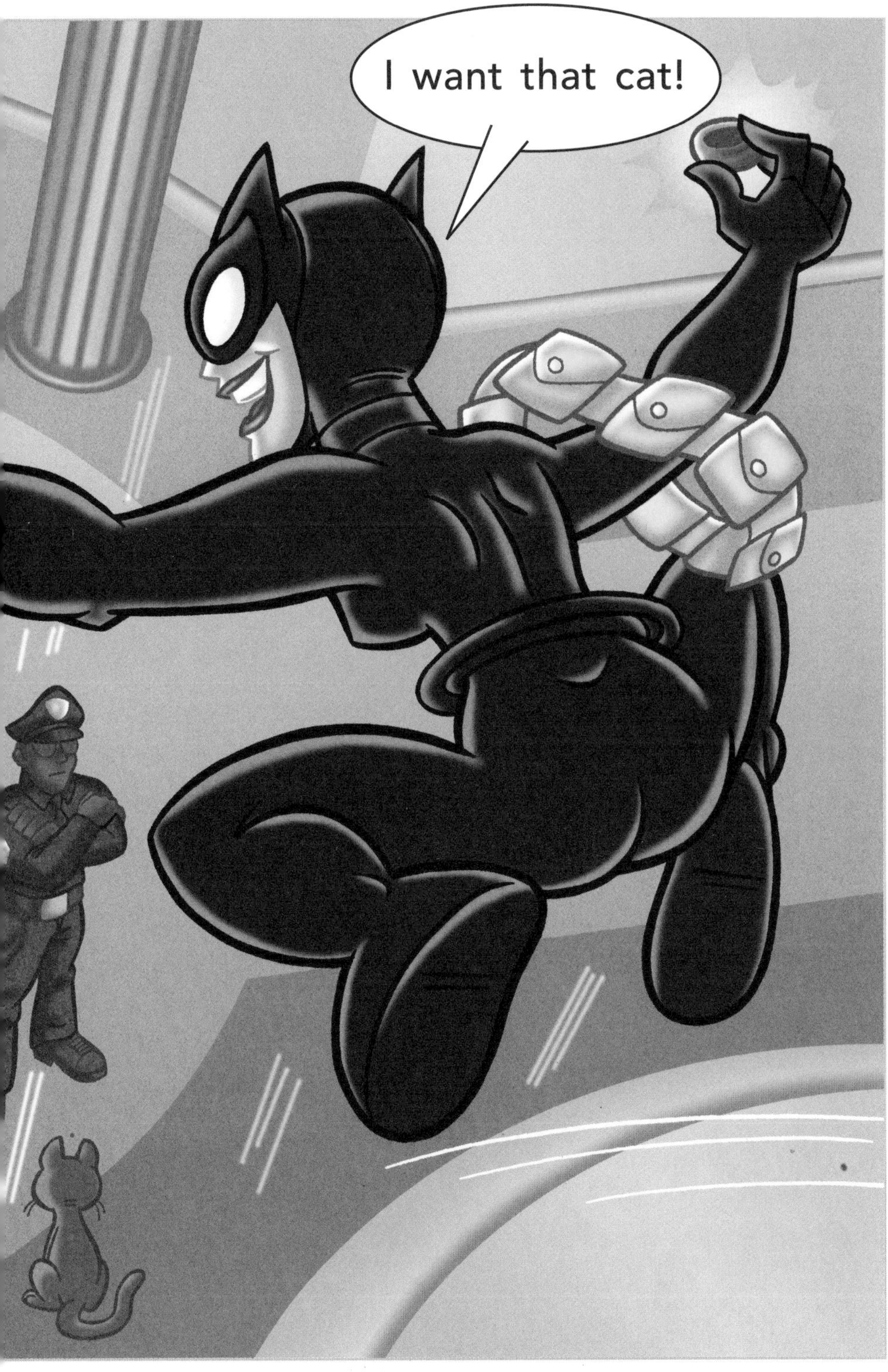
I want that cat!

Catwoman uses Batman's Utility Belt to stop the guards.

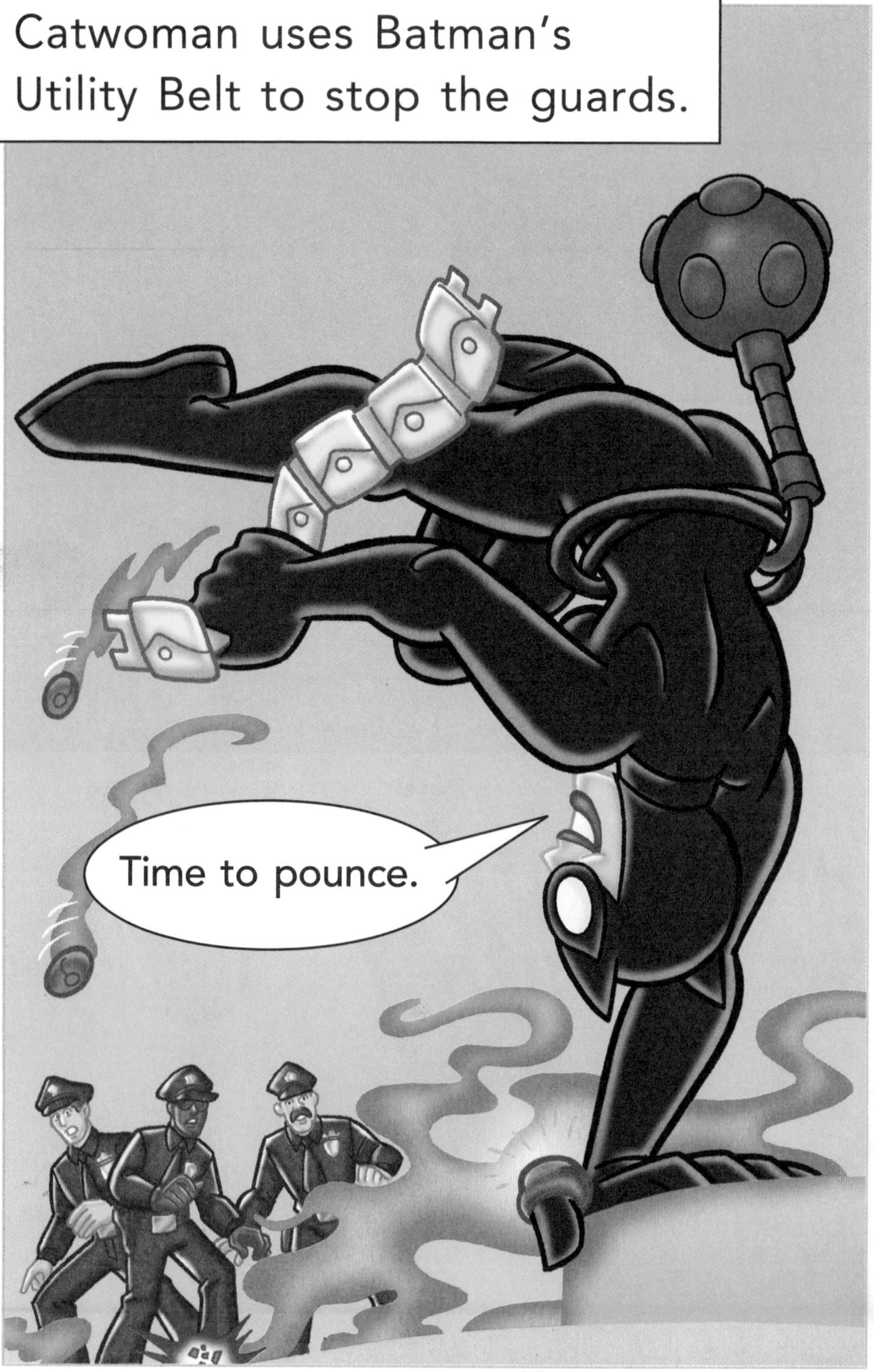
Time to pounce.

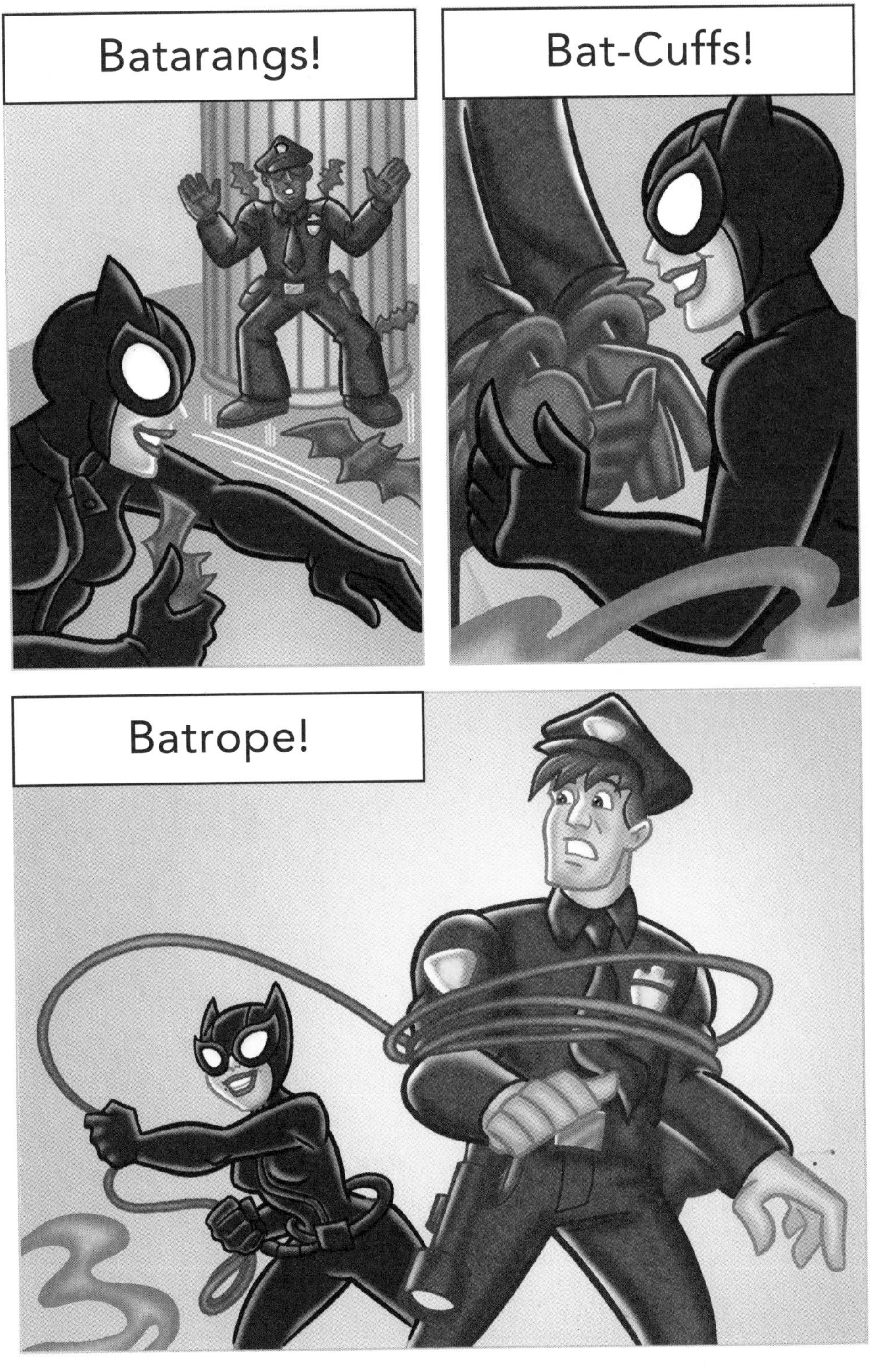
Batarangs!
Bat-Cuffs!
Batrope!

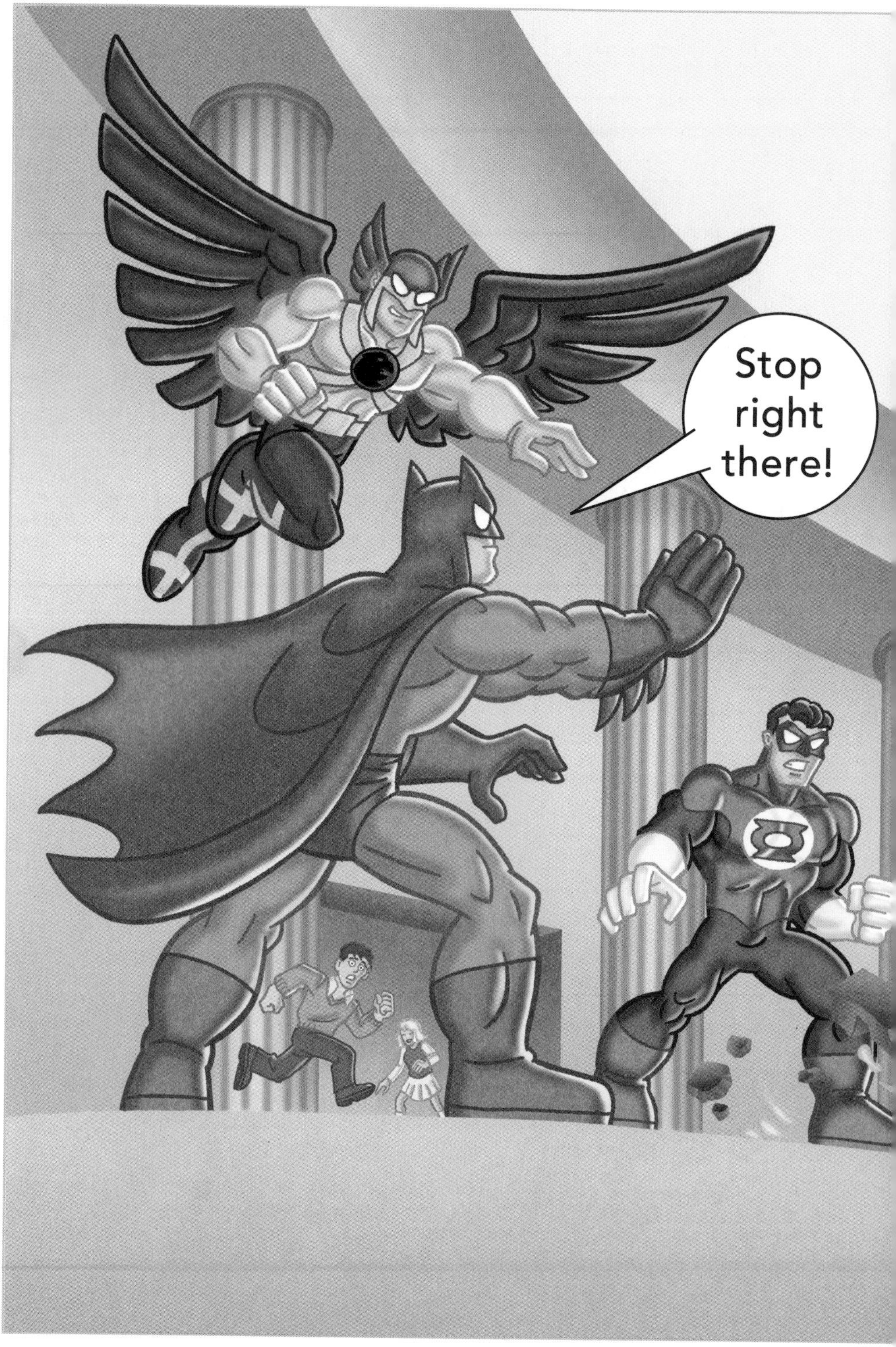
Stop right there!

Catwoman smashes the moat wall with Hawkman's mace.

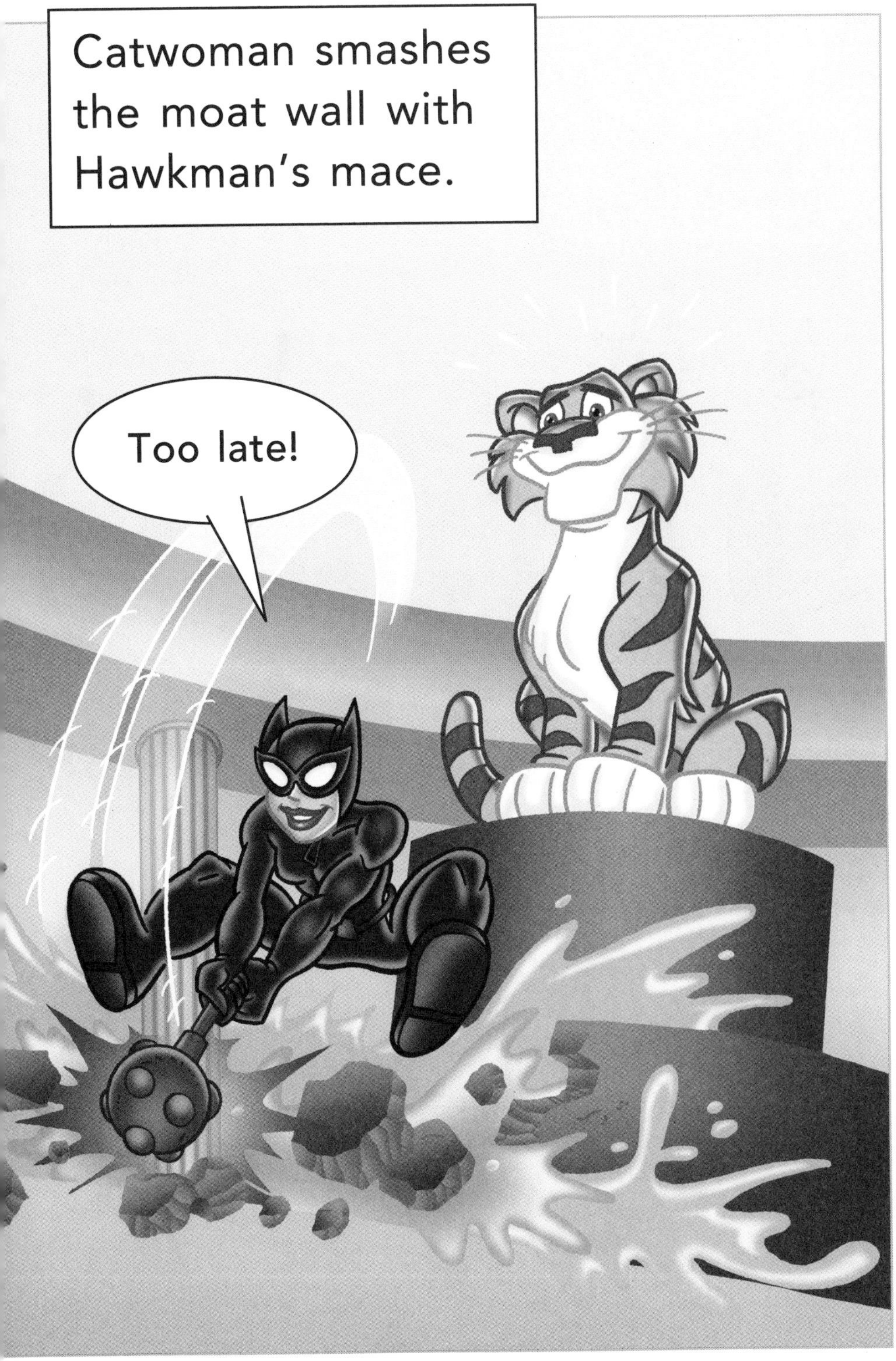
Too late!

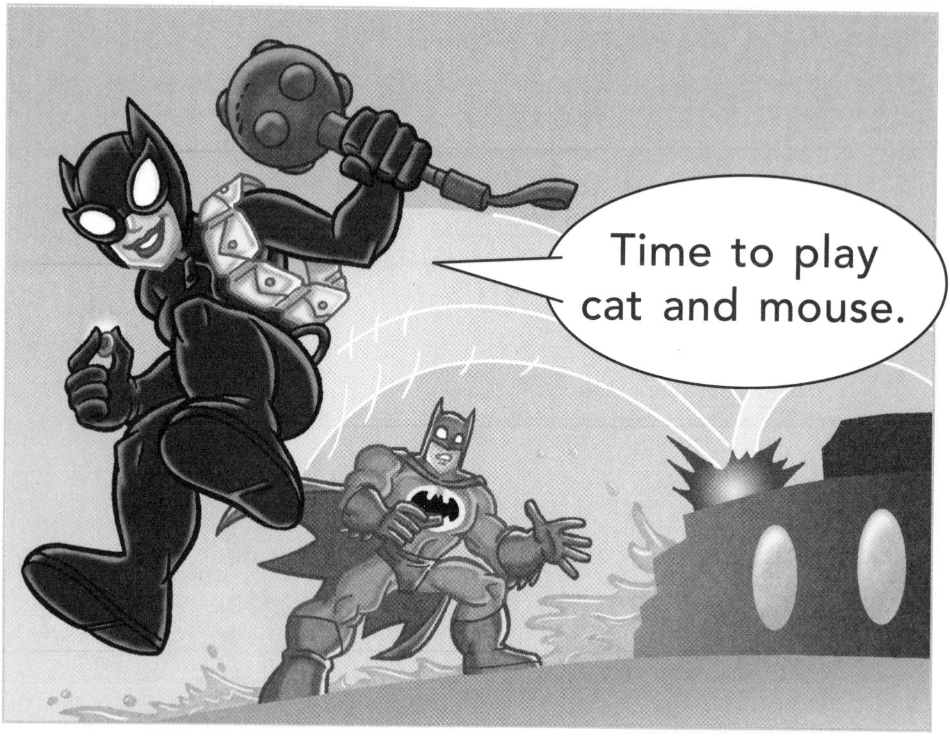
Time to play cat and mouse.

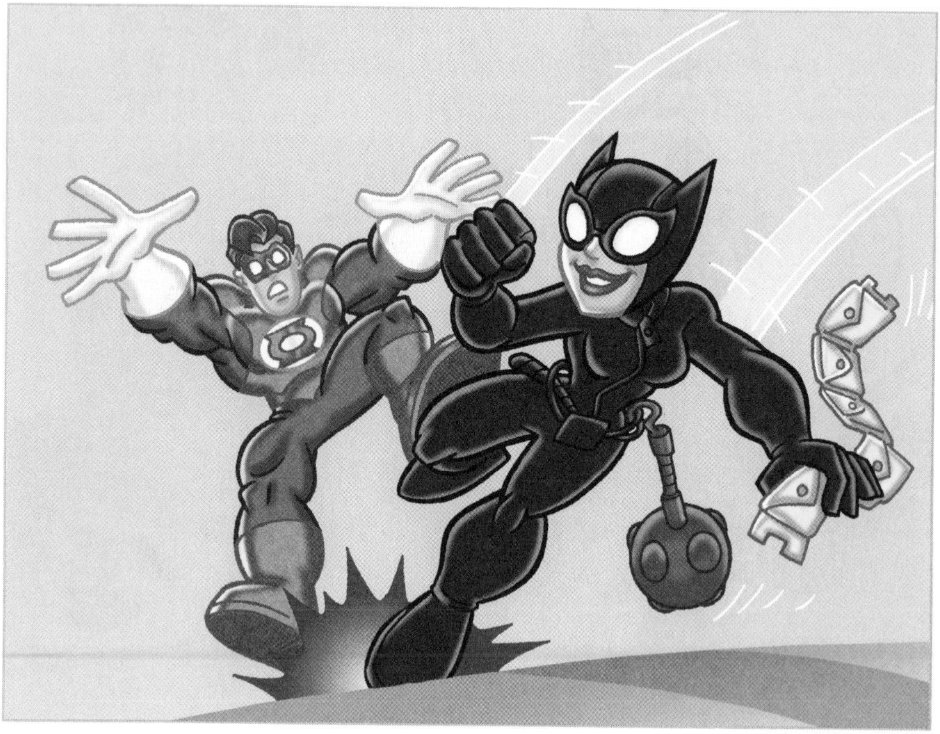

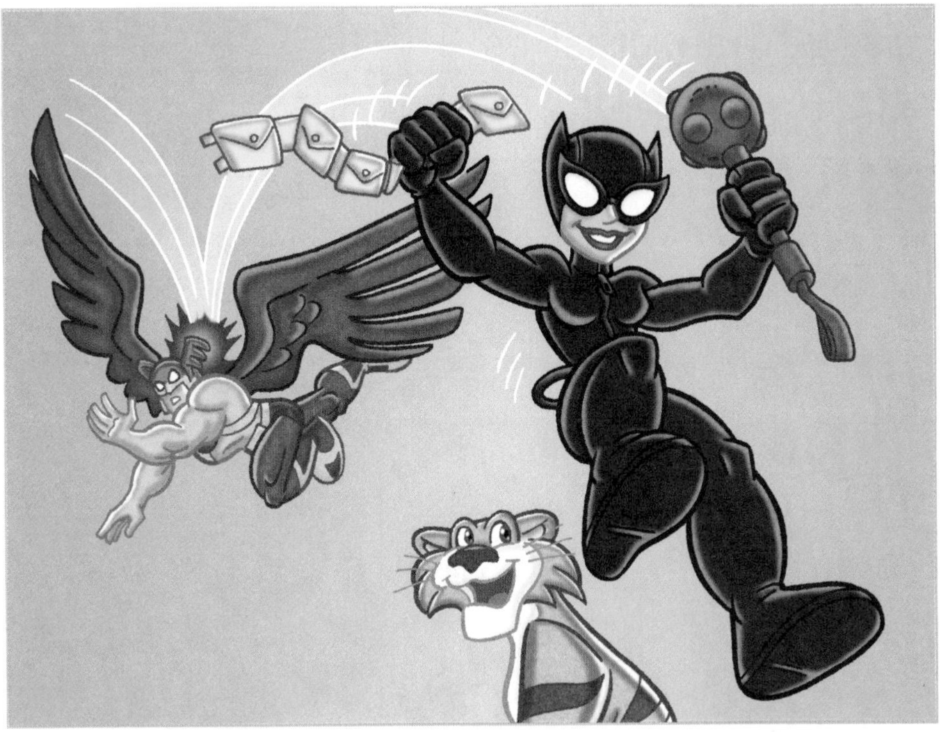

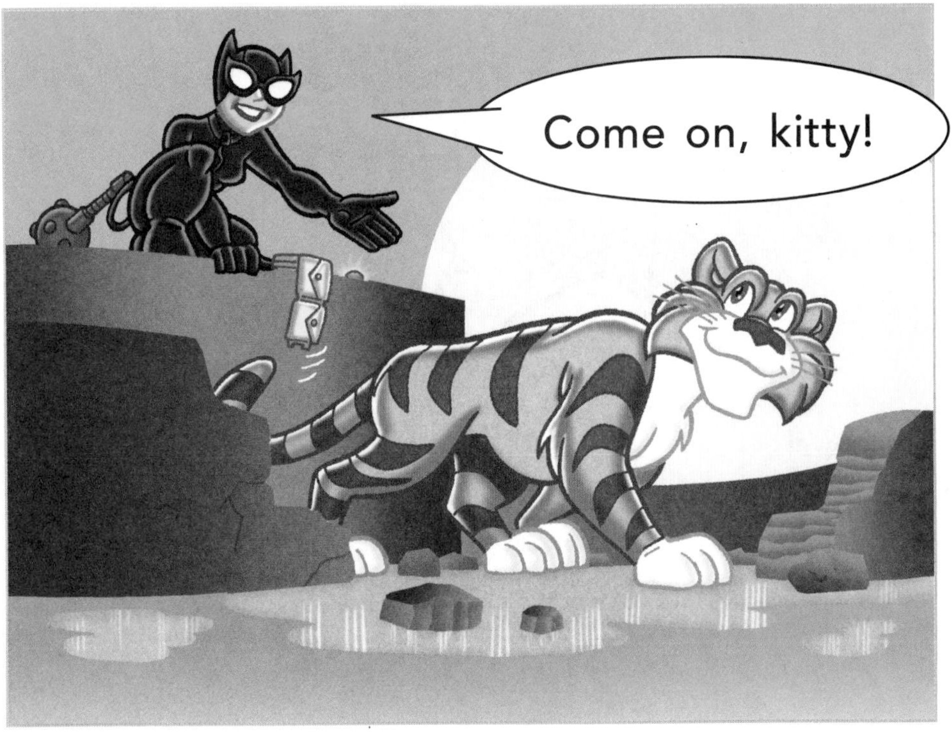
Come on, kitty!

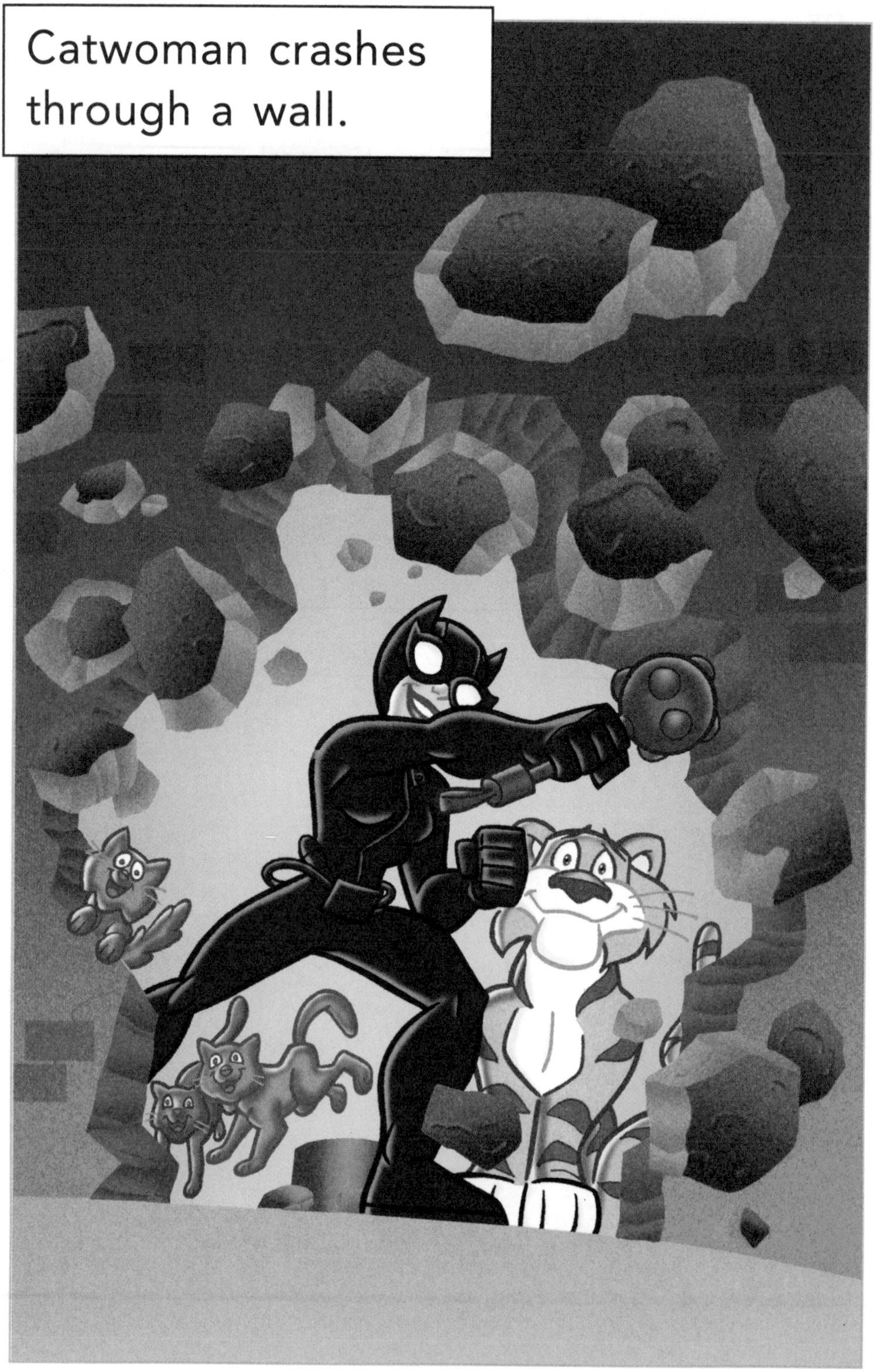
Catwoman crashes through a wall.

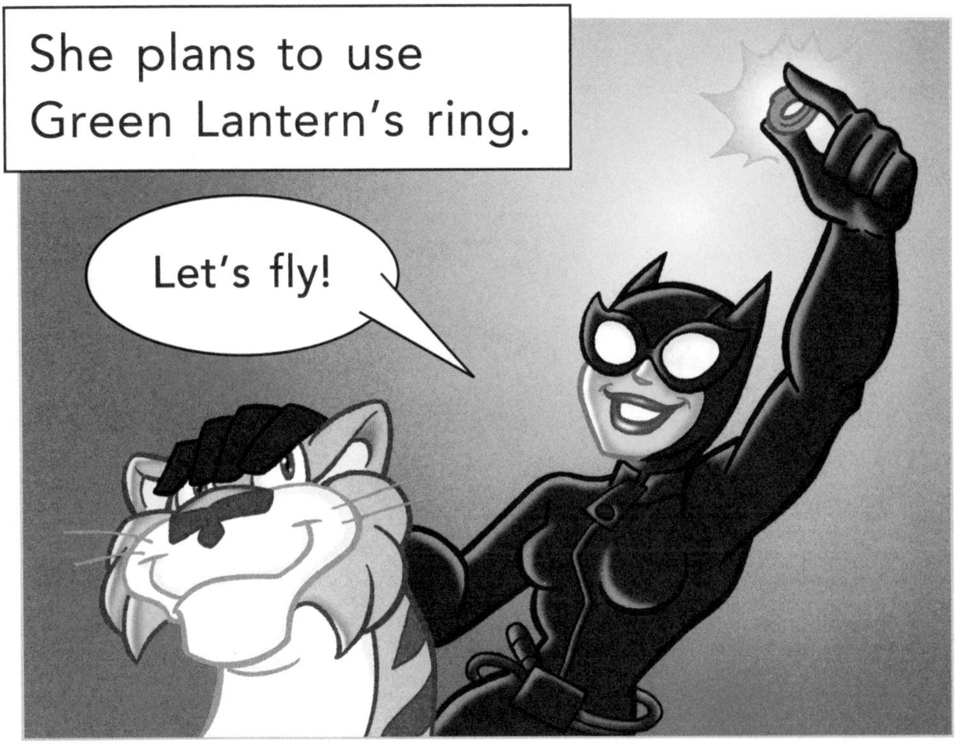
She plans to use
Green Lantern's ring.
Let's fly!

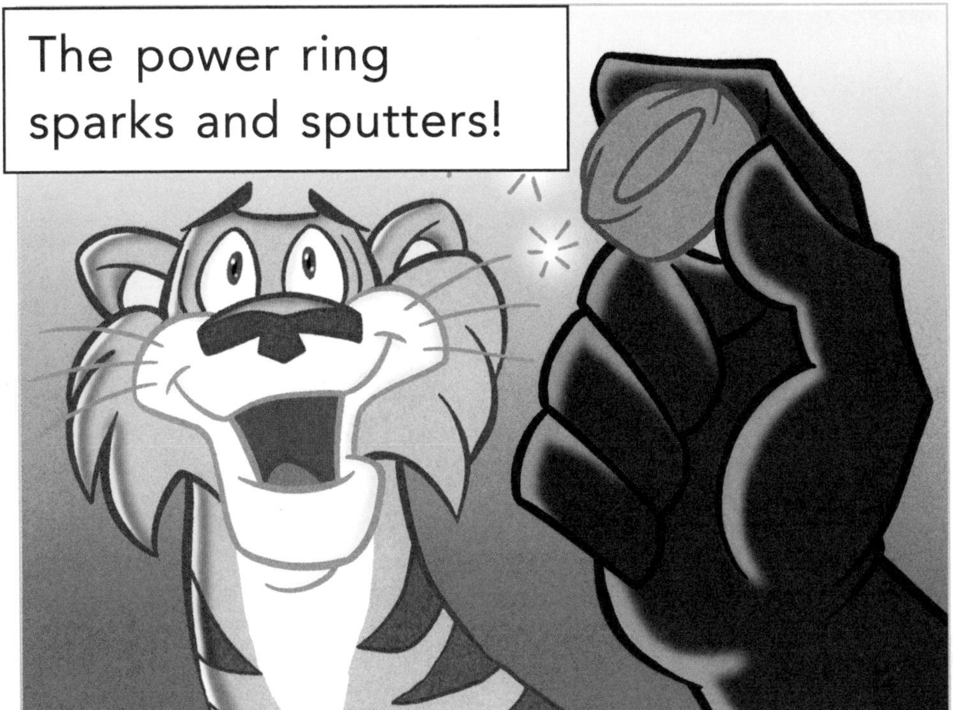
The power ring
sparks and sputters!

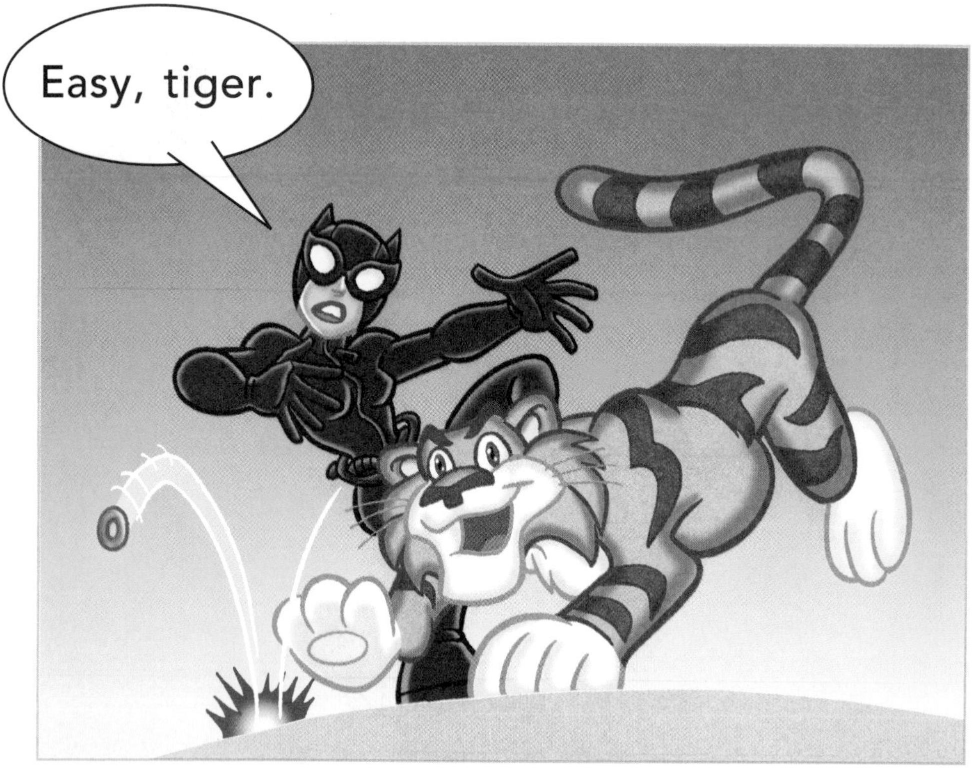
Easy, tiger.

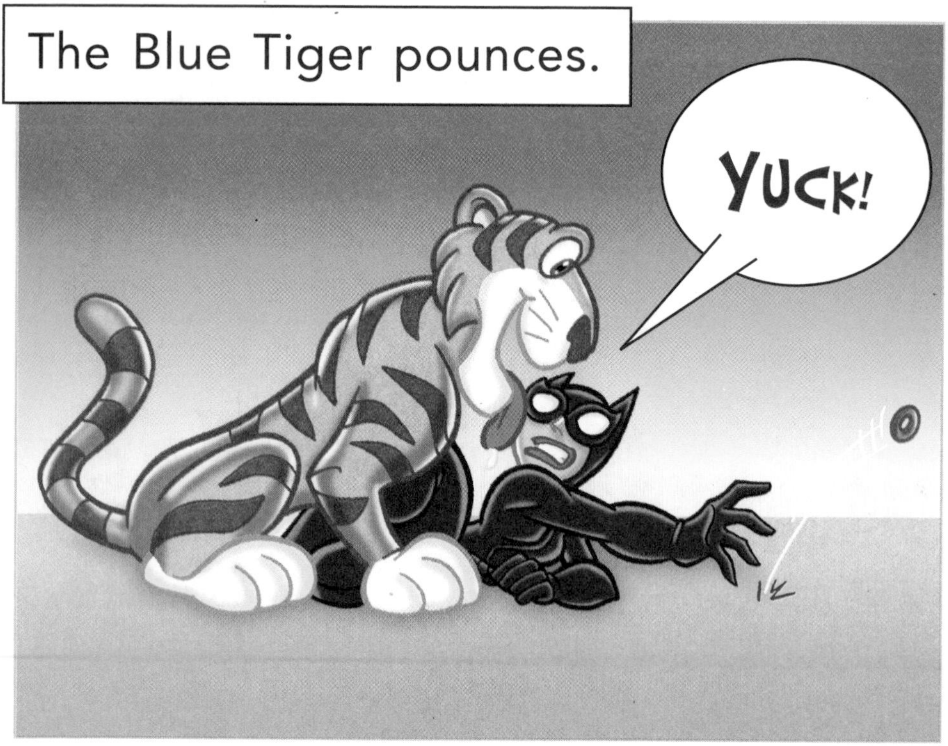
The Blue Tiger pounces.
YUCK!

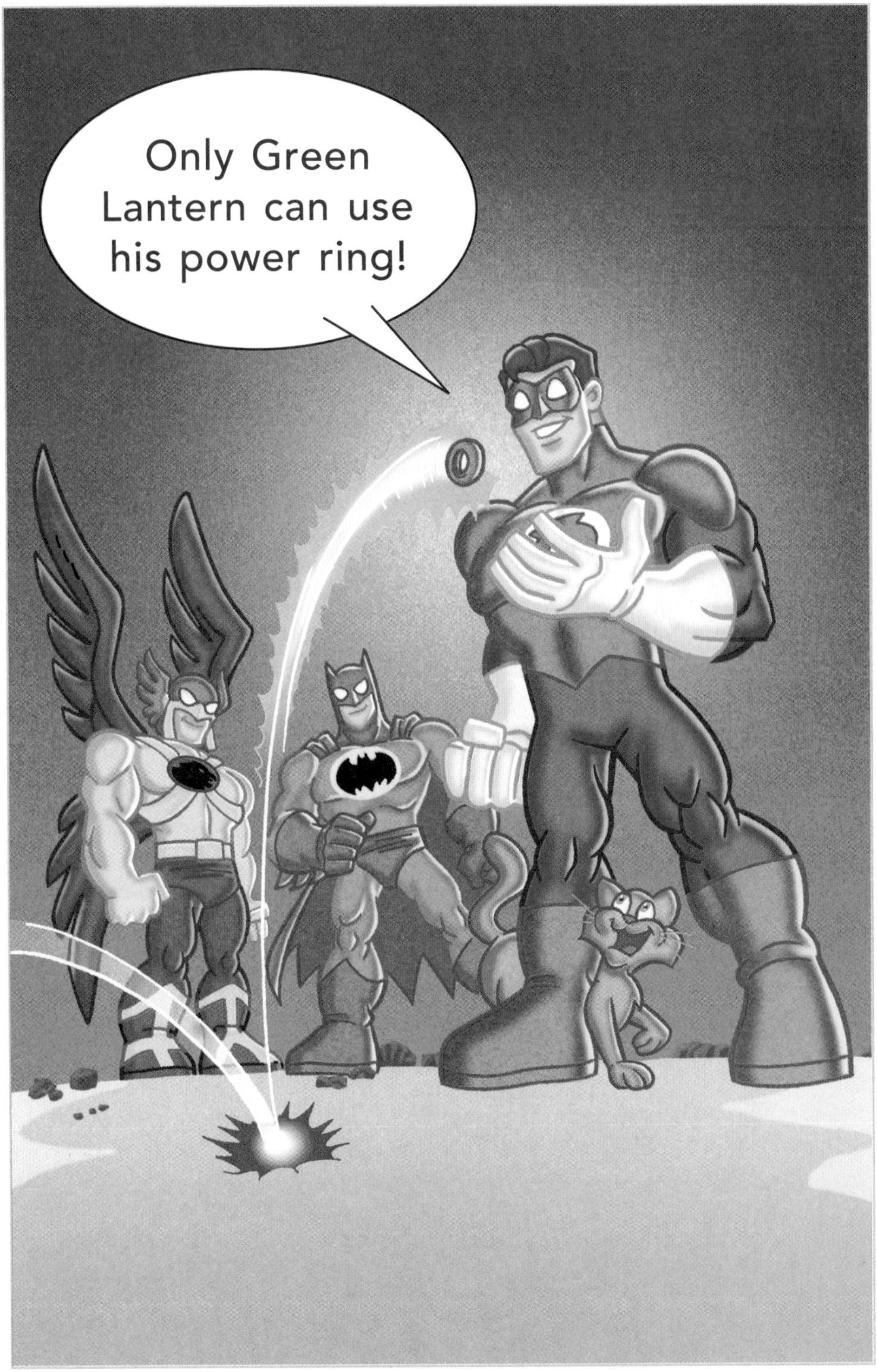
Only Green Lantern can use his power ring!

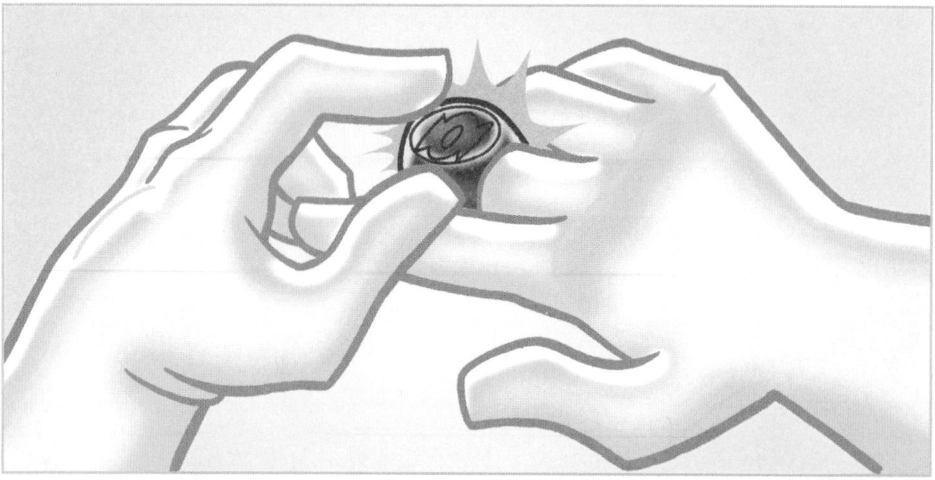

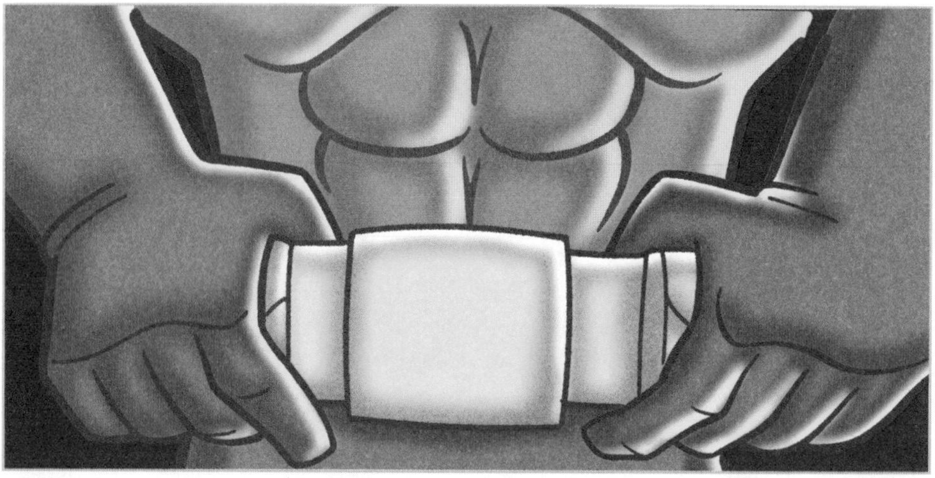

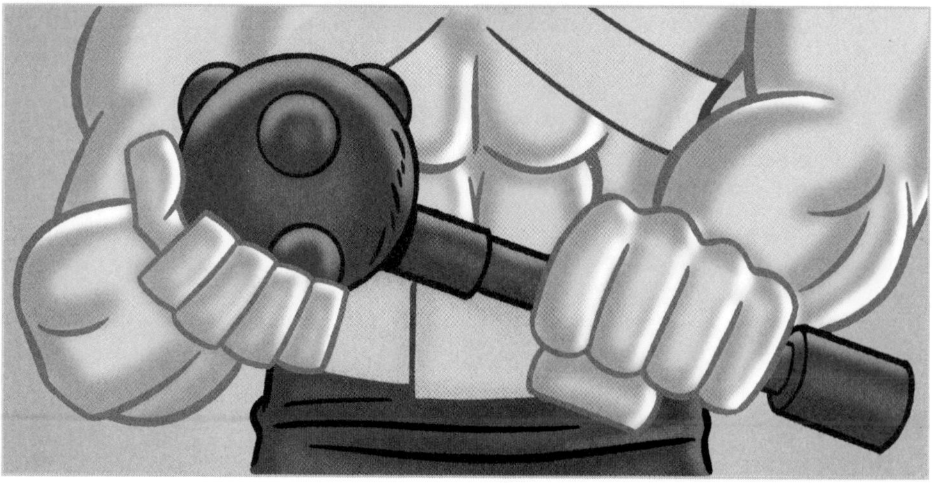

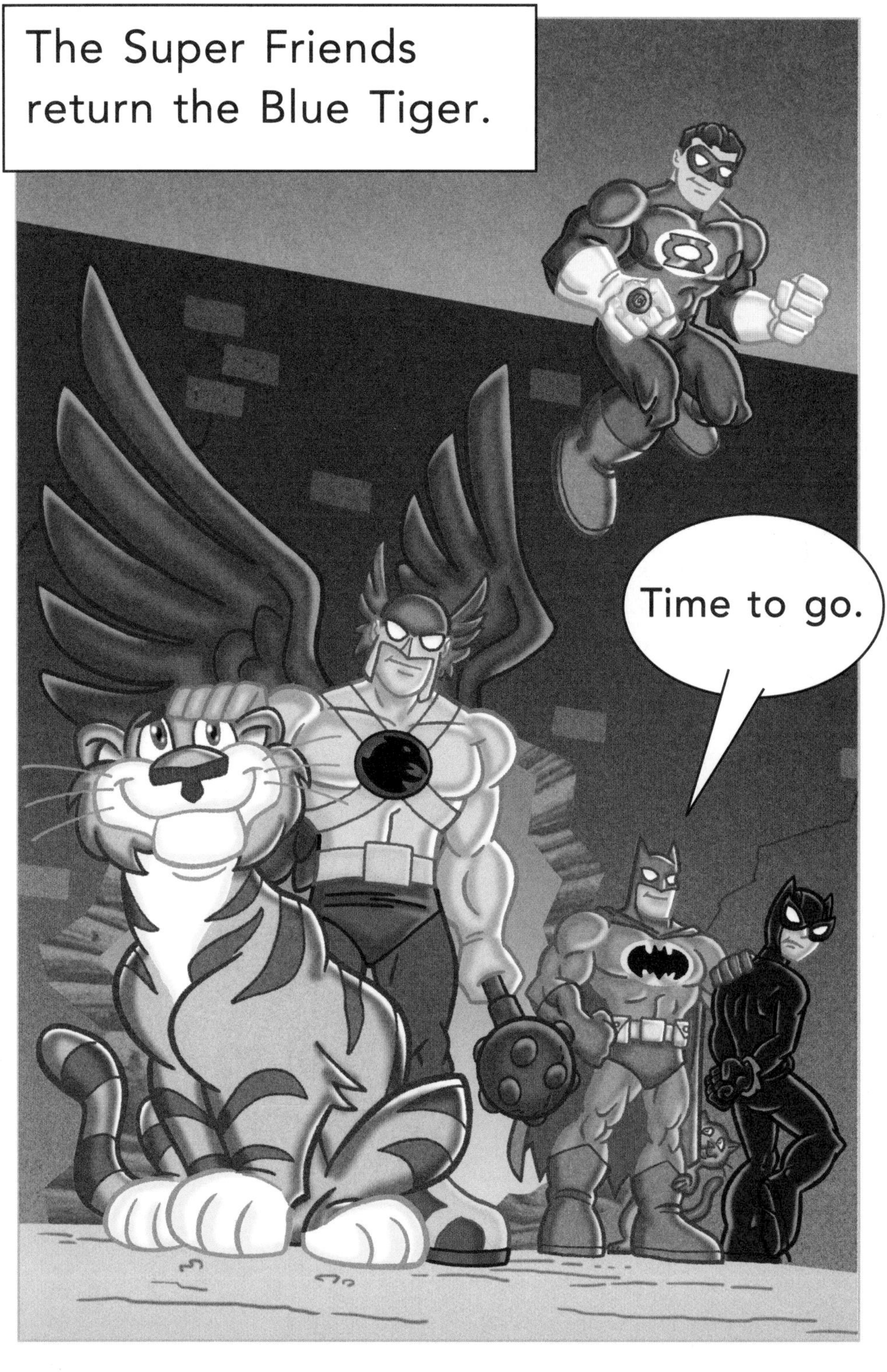
The Super Friends return the Blue Tiger.
Time to go.

The cat show is
a roaring success.

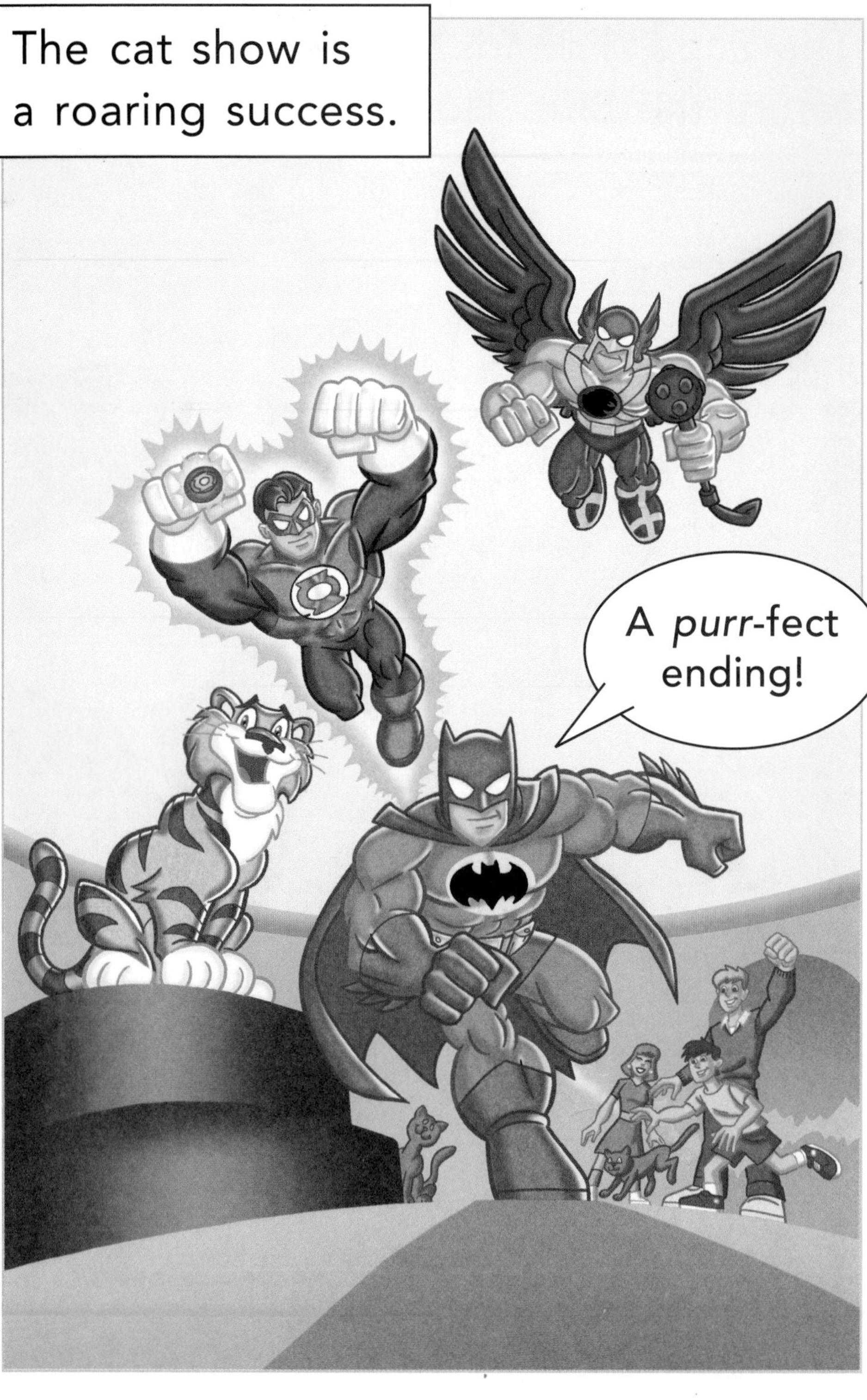
A *purr*-fect ending!